*Samuel French Acting Edition*

# Take A Number, Darling

*by* Jack Sharkey

I0591805

## SAMUEL FRENCH

SAMUELFRENCH.COM    SAMUELFRENCH.CO.UK

### FOR PRODUCTION ENQUIRIES

#### UNITED STATES AND CANADA
Info@SamuelFrench.com
1-866-598-8449

#### UNITED KINGDOM AND EUROPE
Plays@SamuelFrench.co.uk
020-7255-4302

Each title is subject to availability from Samuel French, depending upon country of performance. Please be aware that *TAKE A NUMBER, DARLING* may not be licensed by Samuel French in your territory. Professional and amateur producers should contact the nearest Samuel French office or licensing partner to verify availability.

## MUSIC USE NOTE

Licensees are solely responsible for obtaining formal written permission from copyright owners to use copyrighted music in the performance of this play and are strongly cautioned to do so. If no such permission is obtained by the licensee, then the licensee must use only original music that the licensee owns and controls. Licensees are solely responsible and liable for all music clearances and shall indemnify the copyright owners of the play(s) and their licensing agent, Samuel French, against any costs, expenses, losses and liabilities arising from the use of music by licensees. Please contact the appropriate music licensing authority in your territory for the rights to any incidental music.

## IMPORTANT BILLING AND CREDIT REQUIREMENTS

If you have obtained performance rights to this title, please refer to your licensing agreement for important billing and credit requirements.

"TAKE A NUMBER, DARLING" had its world premiere on September 16, 1976, at the Country Club Comedy Theatre, Mount Prospect, Illinois, under the direction of Ed Sauer, with the following cast:

DUNCAN LATIMER .................. *Tom Ventriss*
 a renowned concert pianist

ELLEN LATIMER ..................... *Doris Silver*
 his wife, a popular television star

GLADYS NURMY ..................... *Nancy Kole*
 their public relations representative

BILL RUTLEDGE ...................... *Pat Moyer*
 Commander, USN, Duncan's best friend

BART MADDEN ...................... *Rick Snyder*
 a biographer for a scandal magazine

ILONA VALDEZ .................... *Janet Davidson*
 a visitor from Valencia

 TIME: the present, during a mild mid-November

 LOCALE: the Latimer penthouse in Manhattan

 ACT ONE: a Friday morning, about 10 a.m.

 ACT TWO: immediately following

 ACT THREE: immediately following

# Take a Number, Darling

## ACT ONE

*Curtain rises on the bright cheery living room of the
Manhattan penthouse of* DUNCAN *and* ELLEN
LATIMER. *From left, we see a sofa and cocktail
table. Above this grouping a corridor leads off to
kitchen, left. There is a dinette table with four
chairs against the upstage wall near the corridor
entrance. Overlooking the table is a large—at
least life-size—portrait of a Spanish girl in a
peasant dress, a flashing-eyed beauty holding
castanets in a dance-pose. Right of the dinette
area is the door to a private elevator; it is an
ordinary hinged door, not a sliding door; it cannot, of course, be opened when the elevator is
away from the penthouse level; it can be opened
from this side by the knob, but must be opened
with a key from the elevator side. Directly over
this door is a combination lightbox and bell:
Whenever the elevator arrives at this level, the
light flashes and bell sounds. The sound of the
bell is unfortunate, a brief and unmelodious
"ptoongk!," something like the sound produced
if one swats a wooden slat on a xylophone with a
tack-hammer; though brief, this sound is loud,
sharp and easy to hear, and persons within range
of it always react to it with a slight wince of
irritation and esthetic displeasure. [When the
stage directions say "BELL" it is this short-
lived-flash-and-ptoongk! that happens.] Just
right of the door is a call-button for the elevator.
Beyond and slightly upstage is the foot of a flight*

5

of stairs which presumably lead up and around
the back of the elevator housing to a bedroom on
the floor above. Angling downstage right of the
stairs is a large picture window, flanked by draw-
drapes, and through this window we can see
distant skyscrapers; a wide brick ledge lies outside the window, and a small magazine table lies
on the floor before it. Further down, a spinet
piano with harmonious bench and a telephone
atop it stands against the wall, and a corridor
entrance below this leads to another bedroom,
off right. Approximately downstage center, a
table is flanked by matching armchairs, facing
an imaginary "television set" just beyond the
edge of the proscenium area. The "control knobs"
of this set can be reached from either chair by
the person there just leaning forward and reach-
ing out toward them. The armchairs are low, and
interfere only slightly with our view of the
elevator area upstage of them. The overall am-
bience of the room is non-extravagant but taste-
fully expensive.

At curtain-rise, it is a Friday morning, just going on
ten o'clock, in the middle of a very mild, sunny
November. The drapes are open and the room is
warm and bright. DUNCAN LATIMER, in slippers,
robe and pajamas, is seated in right armchair,
sipping a cup of coffee and watching television.
His attitude is more of clinical interest than enjoyment as he—and we—are treated to the following, which should be audible from the moment
the curtain begins to rise:

ELLEN'S VOICE. (On TV. Tearfully over-emoting.)
. . . Oh, Carlton, Carlton, why didn't you tell me?!
After all these years, after all these children, you say
that you love someone else! . . . (BELL; DUNCAN,

*never taking his eyes from the screen, rises, backs around armchair to elevator door, opens door to admit* GLADYS NURMY, *a mousy lady of indeterminate age, who wears an unbecoming hat, carries a purse, newspaper and suitcase, and wears a light topcoat; she makes as if to speak, but* DUNCAN *shushes her with a finger to his lips, without really turning his head her way, then makes his way back to his chair and coffee, while the released elevator door closes itself, and* GLADYS *proceeds to set suitcase on floor right of dinette table, and to pile purse, topcoat and hat on dinette table itself, her own gaze locked on the television screen, though she is obviously unmoved by the poignance of the words she hears, which have continued without pause throughout all the foregoing activity:*) I can't believe this is really happening! Not after everything we've meant to each other! Oh, Carlton, how could you! Who—who is she? Do I know her? No, don't tell me, I don't want to know! But—wait—that's not true. I *do* want to know. I'm just—afraid to know! Perhaps it's better if I never know! And somehow, I think, I already know! But— say something—say *anything*—just don't *look* at me that way—! (*Plaintive ORGAN MUSIC comes up, and:*)

ANNOUNCER'S VOICE. (*On TV. Over music:*) We will return to our story after these messages— (DUNCAN *instantly leans forward and dials volume down to zero.*)

GLADYS. (*Fluffing hair at temples, as* DUNCAN *starts upstage toward kitchen corridor with coffee cup.*) I told her Carlton was a louse the day she married him.

DUNCAN. (*Exiting toward kitchen.*) But he's such a good-looking louse. (*Off:*) Did you get the tickets?

GLADYS. Right here in my purse. (*Pulls purse from under coat, takes out long envelope.*) Plane tickets, hotel reservations, the works. One glorious week in sunny San Juan. If they don't have a hurricane or a revolution, you should have a ball. (*As* DUNCAN *re-enters from kitchen with fresh cup of coffee, she re-acts to television screen, starts down toward it.*) Whoops! I think they're returning to the show! (*Dials sound up again, standing before set, as* DUNCAN *comes down to stand beside her, watching screen.*)

ELLEN'S VOICE. (*On TV.*) Please, Carlton, please! I'll do anything you say! Anything! Only—don't leave me! Don't make a mockery of our love! (*ORGAN MUSIC up.*)

ANNOUNCER'S VOICE. (*On TV. Over music:*) What will Carlton say? What *can* he say? How can he possibly tell her the *real* reason he is leaving her? Tune in again on Monday, to find the answers to these and other soul-searching questions, in the con-tinuing story of—"LUST FOR LOVE". . . .

DUNCAN. (*Just as ORGAN MUSIC comes up again loudly, turns off television set with a relieved flick of the wrist.*) I'm glad Ellen's not like that at home! I'd never get a word in!

GLADYS. Would it be a violation of professional secrecy to tell me something?

DUNCAN. Probably, but go ahead.

GLADYS. Does Carlton ever get the chance to *answer* her question?

DUNCAN. Who knows? He's been standing there in shock through three sub-plots, looking at her that way, while she tries to make her mind up whether she wants to know the name of the other woman. At to-day's taping, I understand he finally gets to open his mouth, but she slaps his face and runs away.

GLADYS. For one glorious week in sunny San Juan!

DUNCAN. (*Shrugs, takes sip of coffee.*) It was the only way the writers could work it to give Ellen all of next week off.

GLADYS. Those poor housewives. All across the na-tion, a whole nail-biting week without Ellen Latimer suffering on their screens.

DUNCAN. (*Finishes coffee, sets cup down.*) Let *them* suffer. Ellen needs this vacation—and so do I! (*Sees she is holding newspaper.*) Hey, is that the Times? (*Reaches for it, but she moves it gently away.*) What's the matter—?

GLADYS. Duncan. Listen. You're a great pianist. The whole world thinks so. The audience gave you three encores last night.

DUNCAN. Let me see that paper.

GLADYS. Honestly, you don't want to read it. I mean, what does the Times know?

DUNCAN. It's the Chopin mazurka, isn't it! Let me see that—!

GLADYS. (*Trying to evade his reach.*) Duncan, thousands of people worship you. What do you care if one little music reviewer— (*Stops as he finally gets paper from her and turns to the entertainment section, scowling.*) Okay. Read it. Don't pay any attention to me. I'm only your public relations lady.

DUNCAN. (*Scanning review, reacts, crumples paper, slams it down on table.*) Well, that's that, isn't it!

GLADYS. Now, come on, you're being silly. One little remark—

DUNCAN. Gladys, I played nine very difficult classical selections last night. Eight of them I performed without a single mistake. But did the Times mention the *perfection* of those *eight?* Hell, no! (*Flexes his fingers, stares at them.*) I wonder if I'm getting arthritis?

GLADYS. Well, if you are, you can always get a job on a Mississippi riverboat playing Stephen Foster.

DUNCAN. Don't be an idiot. Stephen Foster is tougher than Chopin! Everybody knows the notes! (*Starts for stairs.*) I'm going to get some clothes on! (*Pauses at foot of stairs.*) If you want to know the truth, it's all the fault of that damned piano!

GLADYS. (*Looking toward spinet.*) It's got eighty-eight keys, and gets tuned once a month. What's wrong with it?

DUNCAN. A Nash Rambler has four wheels! Shall I trade in our Lincoln Continental?

GLADYS. (*Sincerely curious.*) Are they still making Nash Ramblers?

DUNCAN. Who cares!?

GLADYS. Nash. (DUNCAN *goes to speak, gives it up, vanishes up stairs; the PHONE rings;* GLADYS *goes over and answers it.*) Hello? . . . Spanish Consulate? No, I'm sorry, you must have the wrong number. . . . Oh, *you're* the Spanish Consulate! Well, *buenas dias!* . . . Hold it, hold it, that's all the Spanish I know. Try me in English . . . Uh-huh. . . . You're sending *who?* . . . (*Looks left and right, fingers groping in futility.*) Yes, I wrote it down—or will as soon as I locate a pencil. . . . But can't you tell me what it's about? Mr. Latimer is very busy at the moment, and might not like— . . . . All right. . . . I'll tell him. Yes. . . . (*Goes to speak again, but other party has apparently hung up; shrugs, hangs up phone, goes to purse on table.*) There must be a pencil in here some-place— (*BELL; looks up, setting purse down; door opens and* ELLEN LATIMER *enters, just removing her key from lock on opposite side of door; she is a few years younger than* DUNCAN, *very pretty, in a trim business suit, and slightly agitated.*)

ELLEN. Gladys! Am I glad to see you! Have you got fifty dollars?

GLADYS. How glad would you be if I said no? (ELLEN *gives her a look, and she relents.*) Okay-okay, sure, sure, sure— (*Starts rummaging in purse, pulling out crumpled bills.*) One of these days you have got to unharden your heart and buy me some sort of bill-fold. I keep mixing my money up with my Kleenex. (*Hands* ELLEN *fistful of bills.*) Did you ever blow your nose on a ten-spot? (*Starts to close purse, re-*

*members, rummages again.*) Say, you don't happen to have a pencil on you, do you? Those Spaniards talk so fast, I can't tell if they're answering or conjugating verbs!

ELLEN. What are you talking about?

GLADYS. (*Finds another bill, takes it out, shuts purse and puts it back on table.*) Search me. It can't be about your passports. I mean, San Juan doesn't belong to Spain anymore—of course, I haven't heard the latest news broadcast. (*Hands final bill to* ELLEN.)

ELLEN. Thanks, Gladys. I'll pay you back first thing on Monday—

GLADYS. You won't *be* here on Monday. Unless your round-trip ticket to Puerto Rico is on a non-stop plane.

ELLEN. Oh, that's right. I'm so flustered, with rushing through the final taping and all— Which reminds me, I *am* in a rush—! (*Grabs doorknob; door won't open; sighs, pushes call-button.*) I swear there are evil spirits in this building whose sole purpose in life is to buzz the elevator away from our floor just when we want it!

GLADYS. Well, listen, as long as you're stranded— I have a couple of nosy questions. . . .

ELLEN. (*Distracted from tugging at knob, half-turns her way.*) Hmmm—?

GLADYS. The unimportant question is, what are you doing here during working hours?

ELLEN. And the important question—?

GLADYS. Did you really leave Carlton forever?

ELLEN. Who cares about that silly show?!

GLADYS. Which question are you answering?

ELLEN. Gladys, the reason I'm here during working hours is because we're wrapping up the taping session early, and I just found out the cast is throwing me a small bon voyage luncheon afterward, and that means I have to pick up at least one round of drinks.

Hence the fifty-dollar loan. As for Carlton, the instant I get back to the studio, I step before the cameras, slap his face, and exit, slamming the door behind me.

GLADYS. What does Carlton do?

ELLEN. Bends over and picks up his teeth.

GLADYS. Ellen . . . !

ELLEN. Oh, all right. Actually, they fade out on the slammed door. (*This reminds her to jab call-button again; then:*) I thought picking up teeth would be truer to life, but the writers disagreed with me.

GLADYS. That's the trouble with that show, no realism.

ELLEN. Gladys! "Lust for Love" is true to Life As People Know It!

GLADYS. You gotta be kidding! Arson, infidelity, extramarital pregnancies, madness, murder, mysterious visitors, amnesia, embezzlement, and an occasional police raid, all in one happy family's lifetime—?!

ELLEN. Well . . . it *is* a lot to squeeze into a half-hour episode . . . (*Relents a bit, says facetiously:*) And it's been *hours* since I had a terrifying phone call—!

GLADYS. (*Taking her seriously, says hopefully:*) Oh, golly! Was it from Mystique Magazine—?

ELLEN. Gladys, I was only ki— (*Stops self as it sinks in; then, with sudden unease:*) You don't mean to tell me you're *expecting* one—?! And please make this panic-stricken lady's final years happy and tell me no!

GLADYS. Uh. Well. As a matter of fact—see, I forgot to tell you that, the other day, this man called up and—

ELLEN. Gladys! You didn't! Not Mystique Magazine?! They'll eat me alive! Have you forgotten what happened to Harvey Spoonbill?

GLADYS. Who is Harvey Spoonbill?

ELLEN. (*Will gently chest-prod* GLADYS *with fore-*

*finger, so that* GLADYS *backs slowly down to sofa area,* ELLEN *moving with her.*) The Reverend Doctor Harvey Spoonbill was supposedly one of the kindliest old gentlemen on this planet—a fond husband, devoted father, pillar of moral rectitude, the works. Then one day he agreed to let Mystique Magazine send over a reporter—!

GLADYS. (*Cocktail table catches backs of knees, she sits on it.*) I don't think I want to hear this story—

ELLEN. Well, you're going to! Gladys, before the first *hour* of that interview was completed, that reporter unearthed the fact that Harvey's supposed wife and daughters were actually a troupe of exotic dancers who had extorted their way into his house by threatening to expose his criminal record as a war profiteer—

GLADYS. (*Leaning back as* ELLEN *looms over her.*) Oh, golly—

ELLEN. —plus the fact that Harvey was actually a secret alcoholic whose spells and visions during prayer-meetings were really a pathological form of the DT's—

GLADYS. Oh, my—

ELLEN. —plus the *very* interesting fact that the funds raised at those rallies—supposedly for the relief of overseas orphans—were actually going toward the construction of a mid-Manhattan gambling den!

GLADYS. Oh, no— (*Flops back finally supine, her head on sofa.*)

ELLEN. (*Having made her point, straightens up.*) When last seen, Harvey was hopping a cattle boat for Argentina, one jump ahead of a raging mob of taxpayers!

GLADYS. Taxpayers? (*Manages to sit upright during:*) What were *they* enraged about?

ELLEN. (*Gives a what-*else?! *shrug, dismissing topic.*) Well, after all, he *was* a non-profit organization. (*Starts back toward door.*) Oh, come *on*, elevator, come *on!*

GLADYS. (*Will get to her feet and move up after* ELLEN.) Okay. Okay, I grant you the publication has its insidious side. But there's a fine distinction you're overlooking, Ellen—

ELLEN. (*Jabs call-button, then turns head to ask curiously:*) And what is that?

GLADYS. Harvey Spoonbill *had* a guilty secret. You haven't. And even Mystique Magazine can't dig up dirt if there *isn't* any dirt.

ELLEN. (*Turns face away, so* GLADYS *does not see uneasy expression.*) Uh . . . well . . . of *course* not! (*BELL; she starts into elevator.*) Listen, I hate to be abrupt, but the gang will be waiting for me at the studio, and—

GLADYS. Oh, wait! Something you should know. Duncan bombed in the Times.

ELLEN. (*Hovering just inside elevator, holding door open.*) Bad?

GLADYS. Well, they didn't exactly say, "Old potato-fingers shoots down Chopin—!", but you know how sensitive your husband is . . .

ELLEN. It was the mazurka, wasn't it!

GLADYS. Then you noticed.

ELLEN. Who didn't! I thought his hand would *never* stop hovering over that next chord! Poor Dunc. He says a three-year-old child could play that mazurka. A simple waltz-beat and hardly any flats. That's why he uses it for his encores: By the end of a concert he's too tired for the tough stuff.

GLADYS. Oh, boy! Don't say anything like that when the *reporter* shows up!

ELLEN. Did it sound *that* bad?

GLADYS. It *sounds* just fine, but without your loving inflections, it could *read* like hell! Maybe I'd better cancel.

ELLEN. No. No, it's too late for that. Can you

imagine the headlines that would cause in the magazine: "Is Ellen Latimer Running Scared?"! No, you said I'd see that reporter, now I have to go through with it.

GLADYS. Ellen, if it's too much of a strain—

ELLEN. Don't worry, I'll manage somehow. . . . Oh, dear, the time! I've got to get *out* of here!

GLADYS. And if that reporter shows up?

ELLEN. Oh . . . well, I guess you'd better not send him away, but—for heaven's sake—if you can—don't let Dunc find out what he wants until he feels better about that mazurka!

GLADYS. Check.

ELLEN. (*One last left-right glance.*) Am I forgetting anything?

GLADYS. You might put that money in your pocket instead of clutching it in your fist that way. New York muggers are tough enough without waving a red cape at them.

ELLEN. (*Hastily stuffing money into jacket pocket.*) Good idea. Oh! The tickets and reservations! Did you—?

GLADYS. Your husband had them safely in his hand when he went upstairs to dress. Your trip's all set if he doesn't take a shower. (DUNCAN, *now dressed in sweater and slacks, trots down stairs.*)

ELLEN. (*Still on elevator threshold.*) Oh, hi, darling!

DUNCAN. (*Surprised to find her there.*) Ellen—?!

ELLEN. Did you take a shower just now?

DUNCAN. (*At sea.*) . . . No . . . ?

ELLEN. Good. 'Bye, darling! (*Shuts door and she is gone.*)

DUNCAN. (*Blinks, turns toward* GLADYS.) Gladys . . .

GLADYS. (*Gathering her suitcase, coat, etc. from dinette area.*) No.

DUNCAN. No *what?*

GLADYS. (*Heading for stairs with gear.*) No, I won't explain what your wife meant by that.

DUNCAN. You're going to leave me here, stuck with the strange notion that my wife just walked out on me because I need a shower?

GLADYS. Sure. That's a lot more exciting than the truth. (*Starts up stairs.*)

DUNCAN. Gladys, if it's not prying into your personal affairs—why are you headed for the master bedroom?

GLADYS. I can't fight it any longer, Duncan. Take me, I'm yours.

DUNCAN. (*Not buying it, especially since she uttered it with no emotion whatsoever and kept trudging up stairs.*) Later. I've got to practice that mazurka.

GLADYS. (*Turns on stairs, watches him heading for piano.*) By the way, as if you care, the *real* reason I'm headed upstairs is that I am, since you have obviously forgotten, your houseguest for the next eight-or-so days.

DUNCAN. (*Stops short of piano, puzzled, looks back at her.*) But Gladys—

GLADYS. You can't have forgotten? Somebody here to answer the phone, respond to the fan mail, fight off burglars—? While meantime, down in sunny San Juan, you and Ellen—

DUNCAN. Yes-yes, I remember that part, but what I want to know is why you are headed for our room when we have a perfectly good guest room all aired out and waiting for you? (*Gestures off right.*)

GLADYS. Because it's been a long week, and the master bedroom has a marble-tiled Roman bath with a built-in perfume dispenser, whereas the guest room —formerly the broom closet—has a galvanized-tin stall shower and a view of the pigeons on the roof of the armory. I'll be glad to *sleep* in the guest room— after dark when I can't see those pigeons—but this weary old body belongs to the glory that was Rome!

DUNCAN. Why don't you just say you're going to take a bath, like anybody else?

GLADYS. What makes you so sure I *do* take a bath like anybody else?! (*Proudly continues ascent and vanishes from view.*)

DUNCAN. (*Calls after her:*) Obviously you've forgotten our last Roman orgy! (*Sits on bench facing piano, but continues to call after her:*) You could have warned us those grapes would stain the tub!

GLADYS. (*Off.*) Is *that* what those things were? No wonder I couldn't work up a lather!

DUNCAN. (*Laughs, turns head to face piano again, sags as he realizes this is The Moment of Truth; raises fingers to point toward his face, sighs hopefully, and addresses them:*) Okay, fellas, here we go! (*Turns them back toward keyboard, takes a breath, then plays first three measures of Chopin's* Mazurka *in B-Flat, pauses soulfully, goes to proceed, then realizes he cannot.*) Oh, boy! (*Addresses fingers again, a bit more sternly:*) Listen, fun is fun, now let's get down to business! (*Begins same selection, hits same snag.*) Wait. Keep calm, Duncan Latimer, you're starting to psych yourself out. (*To fingers:*) All right, guys, that was just a warmup. Come on, now! *Get that mazurka!* (*Same piece, same snag; he pauses thoughtfully, rests his fingers lightly on the keyboard, comes to a decision, takes a deep breath, sits bravely taller—then begins to play Stephen Foster's* Camptown Races; *BELL.*) Saved! (*Rises immediately, goes to elevator, opens door, reacts with surprised delight as* BILL RUTLEDGE *enters;* BILL *is about* DUNCAN'S *age, very good-looking, and resplendent in the dress uniform of a U.S. Navy Commander, and carries a suitcase and a heavy-but-not-overlarge wrapped package.*) Bill Rutledge!

BILL. (*Setting down suitcase, but retaining package in left hand.*) Dunc, you old son of a gun! (*Business of shaking hands, pounding shoulders, etc., during:*)

DUNCAN. Hey!

BILL. Hey!

DUNCAN. What the hell are you doing in New York?

BILL. I'm between planes. I've got a two-day lay-over in town before I fly to Europe to rejoin my ship.

DUNCAN. You son of a gun! Hey, let me look at you! Bill, I swear you don't look a day older since— How long's it been, anyhow!?

BILL. Gotta be at least five years. The Navy hasn't been the same without you.

DUNCAN. And don't think the government's not grateful! Hey, where're you staying?

BILL. Here.

DUNCAN. (*Delighted.*) You kidding me—?

BILL. Well, you keep writing me that if I ever hit town—

DUNCAN. When'd I write that?

BILL. Five years ago.

DUNCAN. Do you have to believe everything I say? (*Grabs up suitcase.*) Here, gimme that! I'll put it in the maid's-room. (*Starts toward corridor below spinet.*)

BILL. What if I'm not her type?

DUNCAN. (*Pauses at corridor entrance for:*) All large New York apartments come with maid's-rooms, don't ask me why. If we had to pay a maid, we couldn't afford the apartment! Still, it makes a terrific guest room: Small, but cramped. (*Exits, but continues:*) What's in the package?

BILL. A sort of belated wedding present for your wife. (*Sets cap on spinet, will remove jacket and tie and drape them neatly over right armchair, over next few lines.*)

DUNCAN. (*Off.*) Aw, Bill, you *shouldn't* have, where's *mine?!*

BILL. It's a double-duty gift: She gets the present, you get the fun.

DUNCAN. (*Will re-enter minus suitcase, on:*) What the hell did you get her—seven veils?

BILL. Gee, I wish I'd *thought* of that! Actually, it's a cookbook.

DUNCAN. For *my* wife?

BILL. She doesn't *need* one?

DUNCAN. I don't think she's ever *seen* one! Does it come with a learner's permit?

BILL. You mean she can't cook?

DUNCAN. I don't know. I never asked her.

BILL. What do you people *eat?*

DUNCAN. Out. Oh, she can mix drinks and make sandwiches and pour milk on cold cereal, but as far as cooking goes, I'm not even sure she can boil an egg. Anything more complicated than that, *I* take over.

BILL. *You?*

DUNCAN. (*Will take cookbook-package from him, during:*) Don't look so surprised. Believe it or not, we have a little terrace just off the kitchen. In the nicer weather, she has a small garden going, and I do the steak-charring bit on our grill. You've gotta watch it, though—when the wind's from the east, you could get blown right over the parapet. But listen—seriously—thanks. Maybe one of the illustrations will catch her eye, and we'll start a whole new lifestyle. (*Starts toward stairs.*) I'll leave this on her dressing table and see what develops. (*Stops suddenly.*) Oops, better not. Gladys is probably undressed by now.

BILL. Uh—should I come back later—?

DUNCAN. (*Stares blankly, then gets the implication, and laughs.*) Bill, Gladys Nurmy could stroll stark naked in Times Square, and if she got pinched it would be for jaywalking! (*Sets package on table.*)

BILL. Yeah, but you were never very particular.

DUNCAN. Oh, damn! Just remembered—*Gladys* is supposed to sleep in the maid's-room!

BILL. I hope she doesn't snore.

DUNCAN. Oh, hell, we'll straighten out accommodations later. There's a much more important matter to attend to. (*Starts for kitchen.*) You still take your scotch on the rocks—?

BILL. Isn't it a little early in the day?

DUNCAN. (*Stops.*) You're right. (*Hums idly for a second, then looks at watch.*) How about now?

BILL. Much better.

DUNCAN. Great! (*Starts for kitchen again,* BILL *trailing after him.*) Think we can catch up on five years' back-drinking in the next two days?

BILL. Why not? Standard issue in the Navy is a cast-iron liver. Hey— (*As* DUNCAN *pauses.*) Who's Gladys?

DUNCAN. Gladys? Our P.R. gal. Keeps our name in the public eye and our private life out of it. She's baby-sitting our apartment while we catch a belated honeymoon in Puerto Rico.

BILL. You're leaving me with Gladys?

DUNCAN. We don't leave till Sunday.

BILL. That's a relief. After all—officer or not, I'm still a sailor on shore leave. Who knows what might happen!

DUNCAN. Nothing would happen. Gladys is ticklish. Come on, let's get that drink, then I'll give you a tour of the premises.

BILL. Oh, wait a second—almost forgot—can I use your phone?

DUNCAN. (*Gestures at phone.*) Be my guest. I'll go make the drinks. (*Exits to kitchen;* BILL *takes small black book from pocket, checks number as he lifts phone to ear, but suddenly reacts to phone before he can dial.*)

BILL. (*On phone.*) Hello? Who's this? . . . Oh, well then, hi, Marge. . . . How'd I get hold of *you?* . . . Ah! Yes, I remember seeing you when I came through the lobby. . . . Oh, I see—if I don't dial right away, you come on the line. I'll keep that in mind in case

I get lonesome. . . . Yeah, nice talking to you, too. 'Bye. (*Depresses cutoff on phone, glances at book again, then releases cutoff, dials, waits; then:*) Hello? . . . Hi, it's Bill! . . . Bill Rutledge! . . . Yeah, I'm in town. I thought maybe you and I could go out to dinner tonight, take in a show, and— (DUNCAN *will re-enter empty-handed from kitchen, and stand and listen, during:*) Oh. You have. Anybody I know? . . . Uh-huh. . . . Well, listen, how about tomorrow night? I'm in till Sunday, and— . . . Oh, sure. Sure I understand. Yeah, you can't let the rest of the team down. . . . When did you take up bowling, anyhow? . . . Uh-huh. . . . Okay, sure. . . . Yeah, maybe next trip. . . . Yeah, I'm sorry, too. Take care. (*Hangs up, shrugs, dusts off hands.*)

DUNCAN. Don't let it get to you, buddy. What the hell—this is your home town—why don't you take this opportunity to go visit your mother?

BILL. (*Points at phone.*) That *was* my mother! (*Will repocket little black book as he continues, shyly:*) See—I—well, I never date anyone when I'm in New York.

DUNCAN. You're kidding! This is the superdate capital of the world! And you're a sailor!

BILL. I know. I know. But—Dunc—there was this girl—here in New York—a kind of special girl—and —well—it didn't work out. So—now—I don't know— New York has too many memories, or something. I— I've just never been able to have a good time with anyone else in this town.

DUNCAN. Bill. I didn't know. I'm sorry. What went wrong?

BILL. Well, see, when I met Rosie—that was her name, Rosie—I didn't know she was going to become something special. So—like a shortsighted idiot— I used the old "Sam Coleman" routine.

DUNCAN. Hell, we *all* used to use the "Sam Coleman" routine. It always seemed like a good gag, giving the name of the ship's chaplain instead of our own. He used to get some crazy correspondence! (*Both chuckle at memory.*)

BILL. Yeah, yeah, I remember. The thing is—Rosie had one thing she prized, and that was integrity. Total honesty between a man and woman. By the time I knew I was nuts about her, I didn't dare give my real name. How could I tell her I'd been deceiving her all those weeks?

DUNCAN. Aw, what a rotten deal. What happened to her?

BILL. I don't know. I guess she's still picking up garbage.

DUNCAN. Aw, you're not *that* bad!

BILL. She was a city garbage collector! I was coming home from a party early one morning, and she was trying to heft a large trash bag full of watermelon rinds. I offered to help. One thing led to another—and—well—ah, the hell with it, where's that drink?!

DUNCAN. I forgot we had a celebration here last night in honor of my opening concert. My booze supply is zilch. But don't worry— (*Starts toward elevator.*) There's a little liquor store right on the corner, and this early in the day the muggers can't be out in force, so I should be back alive. (*Tries knob; door stays put; jabs call-button.*) Three elevators in this building, and the one that comes to the penthouse is the one all the other tenants prefer!

BILL. Vicarious enjoyment. Probably the closest any of 'em'll come to living in a penthouse.

DUNCAN. It's not all it's cracked up to be. For instance, cast your eyes upon that spinet. I'm a concert pianist. I really should have a concert grand.

BILL. Of course you should. Why don't you buy one?

DUNCAN. Oh, I did buy one.

BILL. And on the way home, there was this pickpocket—?

DUNCAN. No, I still have it. In a warehouse on Eleventh Avenue, nicely stored. My thirteen-thousand-dollar Steinway, pining away in a large dusty room under a canvas cover. I get visitation rights on Sundays.

BILL. I don't get it. Why don't you have it hauled up here?

DUNCAN. (*Points accusingly toward elevator.*) In *that* dangling *telephone booth?!* (BILL's *face shows sudden comprehension.*) It was all we could do to squeeze in the spinet!

BILL. I still don't get it, buddy— Why not just move to a place with larger elevators?

DUNCAN. Because this place is just a ten-minute walk from my wife's studio—and *I'm* hardly ever here *anyhow!*

BILL. Yeah, but a piano is so important to you—

DUNCAN. Not as important as my wife—and if you tell her I said that, I will personally fling you off the railing of our terrace! (*Shakes door angrily.*) Where the hell is that elevator!

BILL. It is slow, isn't it! What do you guys do in case of fire?

DUNCAN. (*Indicates window.*) There's an old iron ladder out there by the window of the maid's-room. They tell me it will support a human being. A very brave human being. (*Jabs call-button viciously.*) Stupid cabin-in-the-sky living!

BILL. Why shouldn't I tell your wife she's more important than your piano?

DUNCAN. Oh—women enjoy having something to be jealous about. Besides, her career means more to her than *I* do. So I pretend I feel the same way.

BILL. Go on! Your wife thinks more of her job than her husband—?!

DUNCAN. (*Tries to shrug it off.*) That's show biz.

BILL. I don't believe it.

DUNCAN. I wish *I* didn't.

BILL. What went wrong?

DUNCAN. (*Sincerely thoughtful.*) I don't *know* what went wrong. Neither does she. We've just— drifted. She rehearses weekends and nights and spends Monday through Friday at the studio taping her show. I tour the damned concert halls. Oftener than not, we barely see each other. We're counting a lot on this upcoming vacation. Maybe it'll work. I don't know. It can't hurt. (*BELL; glad for break in somber mood, he yanks door open.*) Finally! Hang in there, buddy. Relax, make yourself at home. I'll be back in a jiffy with the firewater, and then we can *really* get maudlin! (*Exits, shuts door; BILL stands immobile, then abruptly gets his things from chair and spinet and exits, right; then GLADYS descends stairs, now attired in flowered wraparound and fuzzy slippers, looking contented, picks up DUNCAN'S empty coffee cup and exits to kitchen; then BILL returns, minus things, surveys room, focuses on portrait, goes over to study it more closely, his back to kitchen; behind him, GLADYS enters, carrying open bottle of Coca Cola, stops.*)

GLADYS. Oh!

BILL. (*Turns, reacts.*) Oh, hi! You must be Gladys.

GLADYS. (*Still unnerved.*) Where's Duncan?

BILL. He had to go out for a minute. I'm Bill Rutledge. (*When she does not respond:*) We were in the Navy together.

GLADYS. (*Takes backstep.*) We were not!

BILL. Me and Dunc!

GLADYS. (*Relaxing, relieved.*) Oh! . . . Can I get you a Coke? We don't seem to have anything stronger.

BILL. I know. That's why Dunc went out.

GLADYS. I wish you'd told me. I wouldn't have opened *this.* (BILL *laughs, and she relaxes even more.*) I see you admire our Valdez. (*Gestures at painting.*)

BILL. I certainly do. This is the first time I've seen

her. Dunc is certainly a lucky guy, to own the *original* of that. That is, to *have* her.

GLADYS. "Her"?

BILL. Ilona. Ilona Valdez.

GLADYS. "Ilona"? I thought Valdez's first name was Diego . . . ?

BILL. You mean the painter?

GLADYS. Who else?

BILL. I thought you meant the girl.

GLADYS. Oh, *now* I follow you! It's certainly a pretty name. How did you know it?

BILL. Dunc told me. How else would I know?

GLADYS. My head's starting to feel fuzzy. Do we know what we're talking about?

BILL. (*Points at portrait.*) That. It's a painting of Ilona when she was the wife of Diego Valdez.

GLADYS. You must be quite a student of painting.

BILL. Well—*that* painting, anyhow.

GLADYS. (*Sighs, looks at painting.*) Wasn't it a shame that such a talented painter had to die that way?!

BILL. You *know* how he died?

GLADYS. (*Taken aback.*) It was in all the papers . . . !

BILL. On the *sports* page?

GLADYS. Of *course* not!

BILL. No *wonder* I missed it!

GLADYS. Well, see, last Sunday, he was trying to paint a torero on the job, and the bull apparently mistook his painting for the picador.

BILL. But that's crazy! If Diego only died a week ago— (*BELL.*) Hey, that's probably Dunc with the booze. Maybe *he* can straighten this thing out! (*Starts toward door, as* GLADYS *starts for kitchen.*)

GLADYS. Let me see if I can re-cap this Coke. (*As she exits,* DUNCAN *maneuvers himself through door as* BILL *opens it; he is laden with a large bag of clinking bottles.*)

DUNCAN. Wow, thanks, buddy. I wasn't sure how I'd get my key out of my pocket! (*Starts past him toward kitchen.*) Now stand aside, and let me set us up for some two-fisted Navy-style drinking.

BILL. Hold it! Before I go absolutely nuts, would you solve a small mystery?

DUNCAN. (*Pauses short of exit, curious.*) Sure, pal, what?

BILL. Exactly when did Diego Valdez die?

DUNCAN. (*Gapes, going into shock.*) Die? What are you talking about?! He's *not* dead! *He* can't be dead! He *mustn't* be dead!

BILL. It was in all the *papers* . . . !

DUNCAN. In the *music* section?

BILL. Of *course* not!

DUNCAN. No *wonder* I missed it!

BILL. Hey, Dunc, what's the matter? All I said was—when Gladys told me about—

DUNCAN. Gladys?! Bill, for the love of heaven—you haven't been talking with Gladys about Diego Valdez and *Ilona*—?!

BILL. (*Trying to keep this suddenly rubber-legged creature before him from sagging and crashing to the floor with his bag of bottles.*) Why shouldn't I be talking about Ilona?!

DUNCAN. (*A hoarse near-whisper of panic.*) Because Gladys doesn't *know* about Ilona!

BILL. (*Gapes.*) Your *press agent* hasn't met your *wife*—?!

DUNCAN. Ilona is *not* my *wife!*

BILL. But *I* thought—you said—that *picture*—?! (*Necessarily pointing to self, to* DUNCAN, *and to portrait, he has let* DUNCAN *go, and* DUNCAN *makes a magnificent recovery of balance and bag of bottles, on:*)

DUNCAN. It's really very simple, if you'll only let me— (GLADYS *re-enters minus Coca Cola bottle, and he switches from panic to offhanded serenity without pausing:*) —get into the kitchen, I'll uncork something and we can have a drink.

GLADYS. Oh, good! And while you're doing that, maybe Bill can explain what he meant about—

DUNCAN. Gladys! Where are your clothes?!

GLADYS. (*Startled.*) Wh-what—?!

DUNCAN. You go upstairs and put some clothes on this minute!

GLADYS. (*Hardly one to be browbeaten.*) *Mis*-ter Latimer, when I *arrived* here today, *you* were dressed in less than *this!*

DUNCAN. I live here!

GLADYS. Well, so do I! And at *your* invitation! And if you don't like the way I make myself at home, I'll be only too glad to repack my suitcase and—

DUNCAN. (*Can't let this happen, so redirects his strategy.*) Oh, hell, *I* don't care what you wear! I was only thinking of Bill!

BILL. Who, me?

DUNCAN. Six months at sea! Who *knows* what the sight of her might do to you!?

GLADYS. (*Delighted at the notion.*) *Really?!*

BILL. I never—

DUNCAN. *Will* you take that *robe* off?!

GLADYS. (*Shrugs, takes hold of overlap of robe with both hands.*) Well, I usually do this to *music*—

DUNCAN. Gladys! You know what I mean!

GLADYS. (*Starts for stairs.*) Okay, I'll put on a dress. It's stupid, but—I'll put on a dress. (*Exits up stairs, on:*) Always messing up my opportunities—!

BILL. Dunc, I'll admit I've been at sea for six months, but if you think—!

DUNCAN. Oh, shush! That was just to get Gladys out of the room!

BILL. Why can't Gladys be in the room?

DUNCAN. Because my wife's name is *Ellen!*

BILL. (*Reacts, then points confusedly at portrait.*) But you wrote and said you were marrying Ilona!

DUNCAN. Didn't you get my *next* letter?

BILL. No. What went wrong?

DUNCAN. I guess I didn't put enough stamps on it.

BILL. I mean with your wedding! Why didn't you marry Ilona?

DUNCAN. I did. But only for five minutes.

BILL. Your license expired?

DUNCAN. The wedding didn't count!

BILL. In Valencia? I thought nice Catholics made *unbreakable* vows.

DUNCAN. Sure, but they don't count if your bride's *husband* shows up in the *reception line!*

BILL. Diego Valdez wasn't dead?! But you said Ilona was a widow.

DUNCAN. (*Is tired of balancing bag of bottles.*) That's what *she* thought! Oh, hell, it's all such a silly mess— Look, let's get these into the kitchen and make those drinks, and I'll explain the whole sordid affair!

BILL. (*Takes bag from him.*) Here, give me that, you're in no condition to carry anything breakable. (*They exit to kitchen.*)

(*BELL; then after a moment, the door opens and a pleasantly tipsy* ELLEN *re-enters, a dreamy smile on her face as she removes her key from the lock and pockets it, then does a waltz-time pirouette with arms straight out at shoulder-height, shoulders slightly shrugged in rapture, and head tilted slightly to one side, eyes half-closed;* GLADYS, *now in a becoming dress and unbecoming flat shoes, appears on stairs in time to catch the last bit of this motion, which ends with* ELLEN *staggering slightly, and recovering balance.*)

GLADYS. Can this be the girl who just slapped Carlton's face and ran off sobbing?

ELLEN. (*Blinks, recognizes her, giggles.*) Oh, Gladys, do I look as giddy as I feel? There's nothing like a bunch of actors when it comes to throwing a party! Wowee!

GLADYS. (*Steadying her, helping her off with her gloves.*) Don't I know it! I was at your wingding last night after Duncan's concert! The only thing that kept the guests from swinging from the chandelier is that you don't have a chandelier!

ELLEN. I'd better have some coffee before Dunc sees me . . .

GLADYS. (*Forestalls her move toward kitchen.*) Then you'd better let me bring it to your room, because your husband is out in the kitchen with a guest —a Navy man named Bill Rutledge.

ELLEN. *The* Bill Rutledge? Oh, my heavens, and me half in the bag! Dunc will never forgive me!

GLADYS. He can't condemn what he doesn't know. Now come on, up to a nice cool showerbath . . .

ELLEN. (*Letting herself be led toward the stairs.*) Oh, but we did have a simply marvelous time! A real bon voyage bash!

GLADYS. Where did you go?

ELLEN. The V.F.W. hall over on Broadway. You know, the veterans' club. I danced and danced and danced.

GLADYS. At this time of day?

ELLEN. Well, I could hardly say no to a veteran!

GLADYS. How do you know the man was a veteran?

ELLEN. (*On stairs, pauses, thinks then says:*) He danced with a limp.

GLADYS. (*Viewing this obvious jest with a jaded eye.*) Oh, brother! Never mind worrying about you meeting *Bill!* How do you think a line like that would look in Mystique Magazine?! (*Bustles* ELLEN *up the stairs.*) You're getting into the showerbath, and then I'm going to phone that magazine and postpone!

ELLEN. But you said—

GLADYS. I'd rather have them think you're running

scared than find out you can barely walk! (*They are gone; a moment later, we hear:*)

DUNCAN. (*Off.*) . . . all very simple, really, and not as bad as it looks—! (*Enters from kitchen with* BILL, *as he talks, each of them carrying a large scotch-on-the-rocks; they will move down to armchairs, and* DUNCAN *will sit left, and* BILL *right, over next few lines; throughout discourse,* DUNCAN—*seated on forward edge of his chair, although* BILL *will lean back more comfortably— will dart anxious glances toward the stairs, frequently, lest he be overheard.*) Let me just spill the whole horrible story, quick, before Gladys gets back down here, okay?

BILL. Yes, by all means, before I go crazy with curiosity! (*They will sip at drinks over next dozen-or-so lines, finishing much faster then they normally would.*)

DUNCAN. Okay. You remember I wrote you about meeting Ilona—she was singing in a cafe in Valencia nightly, I was a regular customer, we got to talking, one thing led to another, and—?

BILL. Yeah-yeah, I remember all that. A beautiful young Spanish widow—

DUNCAN. Wait, that's the point—she only *thought* she was a widow! See, Diego Valdez is one of those artists like Gauguin—the moment he gets inspired, his home life goes out the window. Packs a mule with canvas and paints and takes off for months at a time, sketching the scenery and wild life and anything else that wanders by, okay? Well, this one trip, he didn't come back for four months—a long time even for Diego—and finally a searching party went out to find him. When they found his mule wandering loose, and his easel and canvas abandoned in the wilderness with a half-completed painting on it—what the hell—there *are* wild animals—wolves, bears, now and then mountain bandits—so—after three *more* months with no word, Ilona gave up hope, started wearing black and weeping in public—

BILL. Didn't that kind of put a crimp in her cafe career?

DUNCAN. No, she just switched over to sad songs.

BILL. I mean the widow's weeds onstage. Customers go for color.

DUNCAN. Hell, she wore a regular rainbow of petticoats under her black skirt.

BILL. Yeah, but who'd know that besides *you?*

DUNCAN. What are you talking about?

BILL. Well, you were *married* to the lady, weren't you?

DUNCAN. Oh, sure. For *five minutes!*

BILL. That's long enough to see her petticoats.

DUNCAN. That is *not* when I noticed them! Damn it, Bill, Ilona *danced* when she sang. Did you ever see a Spanish dancer that didn't continually flash at least a dozen garish petticoats?!

BILL. Jose Greco.

DUNCAN. Aw, come on, you're interrupting, and I've got to finish before Gladys comes trotting downstairs!

BILL. Maybe we should go out, and you can finish telling me everything safely in some nice quiet little bar.

DUNCAN. I can't go out. I have to practice the piano. (*Sees* BILL's *look, shrugs like an embarrassed schoolboy.*)

BILL. I thought your concerts kept you in practice.

DUNCAN. Then you didn't read this morning's New York Times! Now, listen, let me get back to Ilona— see, I was on vacation, between engagements, and somewhat of a sucker for flashing eyes and shapely legs—

BILL. Not to mention rainbow petticoats.

DUNCAN. *Will* you let me *finish—?!*

BILL. (*Holds up empty glass.*) While you're finishing your story, I could be finishing another drink.

DUNCAN. (*Looks into own empty glass.*) That's not a bad idea. Come on, let's get a refill! (*At that mo-*

*ment,* GLADYS *enters from kitchen, carry cup of coffee on a saucer, headed for stairs; both men react.*)
Gladys! I didn't see you come downstairs!

GLADYS. (*Without breaking stride.*) I came down the outside stairs on the terrace.

DUNCAN. In November?!

GLADYS. (*Just before turning corner.*) I should have waited till spring? (*Exits up stairs.*)

DUNCAN. Remind me to buy her a charm bracelet with bells on it. (*Starts for kitchen.*)

BILL. (*Rises and follows after him.*) Hey, Dunc, one thing I don't understand—how'd you come by this portrait of Ilona—?

DUNCAN. (*Pauses below table, turns toward* BILL, *points at painting.*) A gift from the husband of my bride. Diego felt guilty about showing up and spoiling our wedding. The painting was his way of apologizing for his lousy timing. He thought it would help me get over the hurt.

BILL. Like giving a starving man a bowl of wax fruit. By the way, where *was* Diego all the time he was supposed to be dead?

DUNCAN. He said his mule threw him, and he'd been wandering around with amnesia.

BILL. (*Very disbelieving.*) "*Amnesia*"?!

DUNCAN. That's what Ilona said! However—the fact remained that whether his alibi was true or not, he was very much alive, and the wedding just didn't count. So I left him and Ilona to fight out the details of his long absence, and went back to the cafe where we'd met, for a good cry in my beer. And there at the next table sat the star of TV's most durable soap opera, "Lust for Love," having an argument with the waiter over her bill. See, she didn't speak any Spanish —or hardly any—and—

BILL. Don't tell me. I can guess. You stepped in with your linguistic knowhow, you got to chatting after the rescue, then there was the Spanish moon, steel guitars—

DUNCAN. You got it. One week later, we were both back in New York, and three weeks after that we got married in St. Patrick's Cathedral. Love—it's wonderful. (*Starts out toward kitchen,* BILL *following.*)

BILL. (*As they exit.*) Yeah. You know—if Gladys were ten pounds lighter—!

DUNCAN. *How* long did you say you'd been at sea—?! (*They are off, and a moment later,* GLADYS *descends stairs, minus coffee cup and saucer, in mid-conversation with an unseen* ELLEN *still upstairs.*)

GLADYS. Okay-okay. Suit yourself. But I still think we ought to postpone.

ELLEN. (*Off.*) I feel perfectly fine, Gladys, honest I do. Now you play hostess for Dunc's friend while I get into something glamorous.

GLADYS. Not *too* glamorous. Remember, this man is a sailor! And you know the first thing a sailor looks for when he gets in port—?

ELLEN. (*Off.*) Of course. That's why Dunc went to the liquor store. (GLADYS *grimaces, and forbears replying, just shakes her head in exasperation, then continues down remainder of stairs, but has not yet come out into line-of-sight with kitchen when the two men re-enter with fresh drinks; hearing their voices, she will pause for an instant to fluff her hair and smooth her dress, so she is out of sight but within earshot for:*)

DUNCAN. (*As he and* BILL *come into view and pause before painting.*) . . . so that's the whole long ghastly story, buddy. Now you know why I was so scared when I heard you'd been talking to *Gladys* about Ilona! (GLADYS *reacts with light curiosity.*)

BILL. I sure do. Funny the way these things happen—you've just left the church on your wedding day, and the next thing you know, you meet a lovely young woman who becomes the big love of your life! (GLADYS *reacts with horrified amazement.*)

DUNCAN. And, of course, Ellen thinks the painting is just that and no more—a nice rendering of a beautiful Spanish dancer. If she ever found out about

Ilona—! Boy, I hate to *think* what might happen!
(*They start down for chairs, now, and* GLADYS—*in a
wide-eyed daze—manages to scoot silently back
around the stair-bend, but will peek out cautiously
at them now and again, during:*)

BILL. (*As they sit in their former places.*) Yeah, I
can see the spot you're in. And you can hardly get rid
of the painting—nobody gives up ownership of an
original Valdez! (*Takes large sip of drink.*) You know
something—this scotch is too good.

DUNCAN. (*Both are beginning to show the effects of
hard liquor on stomachs that have not had any
lunch.*) What do you mean, too good—?

BILL. Well, right now, Gladys only has to be *five*
pounds lighter! (*She scowls at him.*)

DUNCAN. You know—maybe we should have a
sandwich or something. This stuff works fast on an
empty stomach.

BILL. What's the difference if a couple of old buddies get a little snockered?

DUNCAN. No difference for *you*, I guess, but *I* have
a concert tonight!

BILL. Then I shall get snockered for the both of us!
(*Drains his drink, stands, reels slightly.*) Whoops!
Maybe I have done so already!

DUNCAN. (*Stands, reels a little himself.*) Perhaps
you should go and lie down for awhile, old buddy . . .

BILL. Perhaps you are right. No, wait—I want
first to meet your wife, while I am still in condition to
focus my eyes on her.

DUNCAN. I am not so certain this is a sound idea
in your present condition. (*His own condition, along
with* BILL'S, *is becoming evident in their elaborate care
to enunciate every syllable.*) Who knows what you
might inadvertently blab?

BILL. And what of the condition of your own? I
am not the *only* potential blabber in this penthouse.

DUNCAN. If I have not blabbed in all these years,

I will certainly not blab now. (*As fuzziness increases, each strives for greater dignity in stance and delivery of lines, with lessening ability to do so.*)

BILL. Come to think of it—why have you not?

DUNCAN. Blabbed?

BILL. In all these years.

DUNCAN. Because I have been waiting for— (*Narrows eyes shrewdly and taps forefinger to his temple.*) —the psychological moment. (*Sits.*)

BILL. Ah! (*Sits.*)

DUNCAN. Exactically.

BILL. Dunc.

DUNCAN. Yes.

BILL. What do you *mean*—the psychological moment?

DUNCAN. (*Blinks, ponders, tries to figure it out himself, during:*) Well. It's very simple. You see. Uh— look, put yourself in *my* place— (BILL *nods obligingly, and both men switch positions.*) Here I am, meeting Ellen for the very first time. I have just come from leaving my bride at the church. This is not a good time to bring it up.

BILL. (*Purses lips sagely, thinks it over, then nods grudgingly.*) All right, you have so far convinced me. This is *not* a good beginning to a relationship.

DUNCAN. Thank you.

BILL. It was nothing.

DUNCAN. Right. Anyhow. . . . The next thing that happens is that I fall in love.

BILL. With Ellen.

DUNCAN. Of course with Ellen.

BILL. I just want to keep the details clear.

DUNCAN. Of course. Anyhow. . . . This is not a good time to tell her about Ilona.

BILL. Naturally. Of course not. It is not a good time at all. (*Two beats; then:*) Dunc?

DUNCAN. What?

BILL. *Why* is this not a good time to tell her?

DUNCAN. How can I tell the woman I have just come to adore that she is my second best beloved?

BILL. Second-best?!

DUNCAN. (*Has to work his mouth a few moments before replying.*) Wait. We are having a semantic misunderstanding. I do not mean that she is a *beloved* who is *second-best*. I mean she is a *best-beloved* who is my *second*. Do you see the fine distinction?

BILL. (*Nods, then says:*) No.

DUNCAN. Good. Then I shall continue. (*Sits silently musing.*)

BILL. (*After doing same for three beats.*) . . Soon?

DUNCAN. What soon?

BILL. Shall you continue.

DUNCAN. Of course I shall.

BILL. Please continue.

DUNCAN. Where was I?

BILL. Over here. (*Both men re-swap places to their original locales.*)

DUNCAN. As I was saying— How can I possibly tell her?

BILL. You cannot.

DUNCAN. Exactically. But then—we get married . . .

BILL. Congratulations. (*They solemnly shake hands.*)

DUNCAN. It was nothing.

BILL. I know.

DUNCAN. At this point, it becomes even harder to tell her.

BILL. To tell her what?

DUNCAN. About my other bride.

BILL. Of *course* it becomes.

DUNCAN. Any *fool* can see *that*.

BILL. (*Beat.*) *I* see.

DUNCAN. And I especially would not want her to think I married her on the rebound.

BILL. But—you *did* marry her on the rebound.

DUNCAN. All the more reason.

BILL. But why? When you explained to your wife, she would see that all between you and Ilona was over.

DUNCAN. But it was *not* all over.

BILL. How so not?

DUNCAN. There were the promises.

BILL. What promises?

DUNCAN. Ilona's and mine. A gentleman does not leave his bride on the steps of the biggest cathedral in Valencia without saying *something* before he goes.

BILL. Ah! And what did you say?

DUNCAN. I said I would wait for her.

BILL. You did wait. Four weeks.

DUNCAN. But I said I would wait a lifetime.

BILL. Naturally. But heartbroken as you were, four weeks must have *seemed* a lifetime.

DUNCAN. Oh, it *did*.

BILL. *Well,* then! (*Dismisses topic, squints into bottom of glass.*)

DUNCAN. You know something—? You are a fell of a hell swellow.

BILL. I am more than a fell swellow. I am a thirsty swell hellow! You have forgotten about my drink as you should have forgotten about Ilona.

DUNCAN. Forgotten? About Ilona? She is all I think about, every time I pass that painting. Could any man ever forget a face like that? (*Both peer myopically toward painting a moment; then:*)

BILL. You are right. She is memorably unforgettable. How often do you write to her?

DUNCAN. (*Lurches to his feet.*) Write to her? What kind of crazy do you think I am? Every night on my knees I pray that Diego Valdez lives to be ninety-nine years old, and Ilona with him! Maybe by then she will be too senile to remember where I live!

BILL. How old was Diego when the bull took him out?

DUNCAN. What bull? You are not making compre-
hensible conversation. All I know is, this is not the
psychological moment to tell Ellen about Ilona. I
must bide my time, probably for years. And then
. . . someday . . .

BILL. Yes?

DUNCAN. I will most certainly tell her.

BILL. You are very brave.

DUNCAN. It's nothing.

BILL. Right. (*Drains drink,* DUNCAN *doing same;
then:*)

DUNCAN. How about another one? (*Starts wobbly
walk toward kitchen,* BILL *following similarly.*)

BILL. Maybe I had better go easy. Just make mine
a double. But stop me when Gladys has only to be
*two* pounds lighter! (*They exit, chuckling;* GLADYS
*emerges and descends stairs into room, still in horrified
shock; then something occurs to her, and she claps her
fingertips to her cheeks.*)

GLADYS. The interview! (*Dashes to phone and
grabs it up.*) . . . Marge—?! Quick, get me Mystique
Magazine, this is an emergency! . . . No-no, everything's fine, but there was this reporter supposed to
come over here today, and— . . . *What?!* . . . Oh
boy, oh boy! Thanks! (*Hangs up, distraught, just as*
ELLEN, *in a glamorous cocktail gown, descends into
room;* GLADYS *sees her, rushes to her.*) Ellen, something awful's happened! Marge says she just heard
someone asking the way to this apartment, and—

ELLEN. Gladys, what is the matter with you? It's
probably just that reporter.

GLADYS. You're taking his arrival very calmly, all
of a sudden . . .

ELLEN. Well, I have to see him, thanks to your pre-
arrangement, so I might as well be calm about it,
right?

GLADYS. Right. Except—Ellen—how well do you
know your husband?

ELLEN. Gladys, what are you saying—?!

GLADYS. Look, this is all my fault. Let *me* send the reporter away. I'll take the blame. I'll say you're too busy, or that I made a mistake about the date—

ELLEN. *What's* your fault? What did you mean about Dunc?

GLADYS. (*Takes* ELLEN'S *shoulders, trembling.*) Now, listen, it's not so bad. I mean, he *did* say he planned to tell you— Try to calm down, and—

ELLEN. *Me* calm down?! Gladys Nurmy—! (*Pauses as a happily lurching* DUNCAN *re-enters from kitchen, clutching a drink; he sees* ELLEN *and halts, reeling, below table.*)

DUNCAN. Hey, there you are! Boy, Ellen, do you ever look terrific! Wowee!

ELLEN. I thought I'd make a good first impression on Bill— Where is he?

DUNCAN. Out on the terrace. Needed a little air. (*She has moved toward him, and they meet below table.*) But here—he brought you a belated wedding present. (*Picks up package from table.*)

ELLEN. (*Takes package, pleased.*) Why how nice of him! (*Starts to remove wrapping paper.*) Gladys, I'm sorry—what were you saying when Duncan came in—?

GLADYS. Not a thing!

ELLEN. But you said—

GLADYS. No I didn't! (*Starts toward kitchen.*) I'd better go look after Bill out there. I think the wind's from the east, and he's in no condition to resist it!

DUNCAN. (*Even though fuzzy, this puzzles him.*) Gladys, how do you know what condition Bill's in?

GLADYS. (*Stops, stymied, then extemporizes:*) Well —you and Bill are buddies—you've been drinking together—and I can certainly see the condition *you're* in —so naturally, I assumed—

ELLEN. (*Removes last of wrapping paper, and interrupts with:*) Why, Duncan! How—how unusual—! (*A*

*little bewildered, says to* GLADYS:) It's a—a Spanish
*cookbook.* (DUNCAN *reacts in terror.*)

GLADYS. What's so unusual about that?

ELLEN. (*Extends book for* GLADYS *to see.*) It's in
Spanish . . . !?

DUNCAN. (*Somewhat sobered with shock, blurts almost in a scream:*) Yes, but there's a *very* good reason *why!*

ELLEN. (*Very curious.*) Why?

DUNCAN. (*Pointing in turn at self,* ELLEN, *and off
left.*) Because *I*— . . . Because *you*— . . . Because
*he*—!

GLADYS. Are you answering or conjugating? . .
Conjugating! The call from the consulate! (GLADYS
*remembers with horror, clutches* DUNCAN's *arm.*) Hey,
I almost forgot—Dunc—this morning—you got this
phone call—! (*BELL.*)

DUNCAN. (*With drunken aplomb, sets drink on
table, disengages arm.*) First things first, Gladys!
There is a caller at our door! (*Eager to be away from
dangerous conversation, he moves past the two women
and pulls the door open, then steps backward toward
women—who cannot see his expression—with shock
and terror on his face as* ILONA VALDEZ, *in a peasant
dress and colorful shawl, carrying two large suitcases,
and quite obviously the model for the painting, ex-
plodes into the room. She swoops downstage with the
lithe grace of a dancer and deftly deposits the suitcases on the floor behind the two armchairs, all the
while staring upward-forward, wide-eyed with wonder
and joy; suitcases down, she clasps her hands against
her bosom and announces:*)

ILONA. Que casa!

ELLEN. (*To* GLADYS, *not noticing* DUNCAN's *stricken
slack-jawed stare.*) *This* is a *reporter?*

(*NOTE: Next general business will be chaotic, so
pay close attention:* ILONA *will, over the others'
dialogue, run to a number of locales, always with*

*hands palmforward at arm's length while she moves, but she will always stop at each designated locale and do the handclasp-to-bosom bit simultaneous with her various interjected remarks; the others will remain roughly in place during her "tour" of the premises, and DUNCAN will master himself into mere semi-shock when he finally manages to get a word in, or out, and ELLEN will be too bewildered by the situation to really notice his look.)*

ILONA. (*To window*—) Oh! *El Nuevo Yorque!*

GLADYS. (*Shrugs.*) So Marge made a little mistake.

ILONA. (*To piano*—) Oh! *La musica!*

ELLEN. But—then—who *is* she?

ILONA. (*To "television"*—) Oh! El teevy!

GLADYS. (*Knows, but passes the buck.*) *I* didn't let her in.

ILONA. (*To sofa*—) Oh!

ELLEN. Dunc—? Do *you* have any idea who—?

ILONA. (*To phone*—) Oh!

DUNCAN. (*Gaping mindlessly into* ELLEN'S *face.*) Sh-she . . . sh-she . . . sh-she . . .

GLADYS. Well, we've established the sex.

ILONA. (*To group*—) Oh! (*Flits out toward kitchen, where she will ad-lib about a half-dozen subsequent repeats of "Oh!" on her whirlwind tour.*)

DUNCAN. (*His eyes light upon book* ELLEN *holds; inspired mentally, if not linguistically, he thumps his finger on it and babbles:*) Cook! . . . New cook! . . . *Our* new cook!

GLADYS. (*Kitchenward:*) See our new cook *run!*

ELLEN. But Dunc—why *Spanish?*

DUNCAN. So she can read the cookbook!

ELLEN. But why is the *cookbook* in Spanish?

DUNCAN. Uh. Spain! *We* met in Spain! Bill knew it! He's a sentimental fool! Spanish meeting—Spanish cookbook!

GLADYS. Good thing you didn't meet in an igloo.

ELLEN. Dunc—do you mean—she doesn't speak any English? I won't be able to communicate with her! I won't understand a word she says! (*This hadn't occurred to him; he gives insane giggle of joy.*) Dunc, this isn't funny! How could you *do* such a thing without consulting me first?

DUNCAN. Because—she—she's a surprise! I wanted her to be a surprise! A *big* surprise!

GLADYS. And I can see by your face that she was!

DUNCAN. Not for me, for Ellen!

ELLEN. But why in the world— (*Suddenly reacts to painting on wall.*) Dunc! Our painting! She looks exactly like the girl in our painting!

DUNCAN. Uh. Yes! Yes, she does! That's why I hired her! Because of the amazing resemblance!

ELLEN. Dunc, are you crazy?! *Nobody* has a life-sized portrait of their *cook* on the wall—?!

DUNCAN. I know! Our friends will be *green* with envy! (*Before she can reply, clutches her hands.*) Oh, please say it's okay! I did it for you! Aren't you delighted? Just a little bit?

ELLEN. B-but—Dunc—*today?* When we're just about to leave on *vacation?*

DUNCAN. Uh.

GLADYS. (*Too softhearted not to help, improvises in rapid babble:*) That's so she can get used to the place—learn her way around the neighborhood stores —find out where everything is in the kitchen—

DUNCAN. (*Flashes weak-but-grateful smile at* GLADYS; *then, to* ELLEN:) Right! Think of it, darling: When we return home—there—waiting for us on the table—will be a delicious and absolutely authentic *Spanish dinner!* Won't that be a *treat?!*

ELLEN. After *San Juan?!*

ILONA. (*Bursts back into room from kitchen, flings her arms about* DUNCAN'S *waist from behind, pillowing her cheek on his back.*) Oh-oh-oh! *Esta magnifico! Que bonita casa! Me gusta, me gusta!*

ELLEN. Dunc—why is our cook embracing you that way—?!

DUNCAN. (*Trying to pry* ILONA'S *arms from his stomach, croaks:*) I'm paying her a fortune! (*PHONE rings.*)

GLADYS. Oh, no. Not now. (*As she goes to phone, pleads ceilingward:*) Dear God, please, not now! (*Grabs up phone.*) Hello—?

DUNCAN. (*Finally getting* ILONA'S *arms off him, turning and holding her wrists at her sides to prevent her from a frontal embrace.*) What not now? Gladys, for heaven's sake, who *else* is coming?!

GLADYS. (*On phone.*) Thanks, Marge! (*Hangs up, while replying wearily to* DUNCAN:) A reporter from Mystique Magazine! He's on his way up now!

DUNCAN. (*Drops* ILONA'S *wrists, whirls and grasps* ELLEN'S *shoulders.*) He's heard about the mazurka! (*Releases* ELLEN, *starts for spinet.*) Quick, help me hide the piano!

ELLEN. (*Watching him, does not see* BILL—*still amiably plastered—wobble in from kitchen and stop below table, swaying.*) Duncan Latimer, you are drunk as a skunk! Forget the silly piano, and explain this woman!

DUNCAN. (*Turns, halfway to spinet, to face her.*) I tell you, she's nothing but a cook!

ELLEN. Don't hand me that garbage—!

BILL. (*Reacts to term, stares at her back, wide-eyed, then cries:*) Rosie!

ELLEN. (*Whirls, aghast, and staggers back a step in shock.*) Sam Coleman!

DUNCAN. What—?! (*BELL.*) The reporter!

ELLEN. Oh no! Not that!

GLADYS. (*Who, from* BILL'S *shout, has gone resignedly calm, and has walked to table and picked up* DUNCAN'S *drink.*) Ellen, do you remember earlier today, when I said your television soap opera wasn't true to life—?

ELLEN. (*Sagging in despair, replies perfunctorily.*) Yes . . . ?

GLADYS. Well, you can send me to bed without my supper. (*And as* BILL *still sways in place smiling with joy, and* ILONA *looks curiously at him, at* ELLEN, *and at* DUNCAN, *and* DUNCAN *and* ELLEN *simply stand rooted where they are,* GLADYS *calmly but purposefully begins to drain* DUNCAN's *drink to the very bottom, as—*)

*THE CURTAIN FALLS*

# ACT TWO

*Curtain rises on same tableau that closed Act One, all
persons in same stances and attitudes. GLADYS,
her head back and tumbler tilted, is just finishing DUNCAN's drink. She finishes and sets it on
table, as there comes a KNOCKING at door. All
but GLADYS instantly look that way.*

BILL. (*Amiably drunk.*) Hey, there's somebody at
the door!

GLADYS. (*Taking his arm.*) Three cheers for the
Navy! Come on, sailor—anchors aweigh and full
speed astern! (*Starts towing him out to kitchen.*)

ELLEN. Gladys! What are we going to do?!

GLADYS. (*Still backing off, towing a reluctant BILL.*)
I'll drag the Navy and a pot of coffee up the terrace
stairs. Duncan, you get Miss Jalapeño hidden in the
maid's-room. Ellen, you count ten to let us get clear
of Ground Zero, then let the man in. Got it?

BILL. But I wanna talk to Rosie—!

GLADYS. (*Dragging him from view toward kitchen.*)
Later, later!

DUNCAN. (*Calls after vanishing BILL.*) You can
help her take out the garbage! (ELLEN *reacts, turns to
him with fire in her eyes, but he is already signaling*
ILONA.) *Segue me, con sus equipajes!* (*Starts off
right.*)

ILONA. (*Obediently grabbing up luggage and following after him.*) *Si, Duncan!* (*She pronounces his name*
"*Doon-kahn.*")

ELLEN. (*Echoing pronunciation.*) "Duncan"?

DUNCAN. Well—it's my *name*, isn't it!? (*To* ILONA,
*impatiently.*) *Andale! Pronto!* (*They vanish off right,
just as KNOCKING repeats at door;* ELLEN *reaches*

45

*for knob, then recoils as* GLADYS *dashes in from left
and grabs up empty glasses from table.*)

GLADYS. I *can't* think of *everything!* (*Gallops off
left with glasses;* ELLEN *recovers herself, forges a
bright smile, and opens door;* BART MADDEN *enters,
preceded by a hand-held microphone whose cord is
attached to a shoulder-slung cassette recorder; he is
well dressed, wiry of build, shrewdly intelligent, about
40, and is the epitome of all that is bad about TV-
game-show hosts.*)

(*NOTE: In* BART's *dialogue, all passages in quotation
marks are spoken directly into the microphone;
for the rest, as long as he is carrying the microphone, he holds it to the person speaking, or to
himself, as dialogue progresses, just as in a man-
on-the-street interview; his thrust toward interviewees is almost like a rapier-lunge, calculated
to keep them as much physically off-balance as
mentally.*)

BART. (*Will enter, letting door shut behind him, and
move downstage right, step by relentless step,* ELLEN
*backing away before him.*) "When the door was finally
opened, I found myself in the presence of Ellen Latimer herself. There was no sign of the person or persons whose muffled voices and thundering footfalls
I had heard a moment before. Miss Latimer seemed
startled, distraught, and beneath her lovely smile I
detected something of a strain." (ELLEN *abruptly
backs into spinet, catching herself with heels of hands
on keyboard, producing a jangling discord of sound.*)
Hi, there! I'm Bart Madden of Mystique Magazine!
(*Voice shifts to narrative style for:*) "I said, wondering why she needed to support herself upon the piano
at this hour of the day." (ELLEN *immediately
straightens up, nervously dusts off hands.*) "Could it
be symbolic, I wondered, of the fact that much of her

support came from the labors of her concert-pianist husband?" (*Thrusts microphone at* ELLEN.)

ELLEN. (*Voice unnatural and high with tension.*) H-how do you do!

BART. "—she said, her voice unnatural and high with tension."

ELLEN. (*More normal range, irritation starting to overcome fear.*) Well, if you'd stop poking that *microphone* into my face—!

BART. "Delete that last line." (*Covers head of microphone, speaks with lowered voice.*) Really, Miss Latimer! You're not supposed to mention the microphone! My secretary transcribes these tapes verbatim, and it's supposed to read as if I wrote it all down after the fact!

ELLEN. Why *don't* you?

BART. Because first impressions are the best, and I might not remember all the specifics, later. (GLADYS *appears, descending stairs, will come down behind* BART, *listening intently, during:*) Now, let's get back to the interview, shall we? (*Uncovers microphone, speaks into it.*) I can't help wondering, Miss Latimer, what all the ruckus was as I waited to be admitted.

ELLEN. Wh-what ruckus? I'm afraid I don't understand . . . ?

BART. "I wasn't so sure she didn't understand—but there was obviously one bit of truth to her statement: She *was* afraid!"

ELLEN. Don't be ridiculous!

BART. "—she said, when I questioned her uneasy attitude"

ELLEN. I am not uneasy, and I have nothing to hide!

BART. Did I *say* you had anything to hide—?

ELLEN. Uh—well—*no* . . . but . . .

BART. Then why should you bring the topic up? "Obviously, there was more to this situation than immediately met the eye. I determined to go a bit further."

GLADYS. (*Takes microphone from his hand before he realizes her presence, and whimpers into it in a plaintive falsetto:*) No, Mister Madden! Stop! What are you doing! Oh, you've torn my dress off! Help! Police! Sex maniac!

BART. (*Frantically grabs microphone back.*) Good grief, what are you doing?!

GLADYS. Giving your secretary an earful.

BART. Damn it all, now I'll have to run the tape back and erase it myself! Who the hell *are* you, anyway?!

GLADYS. I'm one of the thundering footfalls you heard before Ellen let you in. Didn't you ever hear of straightening up a room for company, you creep?!

BART. "Whoever this newcomer was, I told myself, she was patently short on manners and vocabulary."

GLADYS. Why, you dirty—!

ELLEN. Gladys—!

BART. "—Miss Latimer cried frantically. But now I knew I was in the presence of none other than Gladys Nurmy, the public relations representative for the star of 'Lust for Love' and for Duncan Latimer, her famous spouse."

GLADYS. Oh, boy! I'm beginning to understand what happened to Harvey Spoonbill!

BART. Ah! Then you were acquainted with that famous fraud? How well did you know him?

GLADYS. I never even *heard* of him till *Ellen* told me—

ELLEN. (*Sensing doom.*) Uh—now—Gladys—!

BART. "—said Ellen Latimer, her tone ill-concealing a hidden warning. It was becoming plain that the TV star herself had had more-than-casual knowledge of that infamous man, who, posing as an honest evangelist—"

GLADYS. (*Grabbing microphone.*) —became the father of an illegitimate son named Bart Madden!

BART. (*Wrestling with microphone, trying to get it back.*) Let go! I warn you, this is personal property—!

GLADYS. Well, so is Ellen's reputation! (*Lets go, suddenly, so that he staggers back.*)

BART. I had no intention of—

ELLEN. The hell you didn't!

BART. Listen—

ELLEN. No, you listen! You're here for a full-length feature about me. I'm sure your employer expects no less— (*Raises palm toward him, forestalling his upcoming interruption.*) —and I'm *just* as sure you haven't got more than a paragraph on that tape, yet. I'm willing to gamble it's not enough for you to bring back without getting into trouble, right—?!

GLADYS. Of course you're right! Throw the bum out now, and he's in more trouble than you can shake a stick at.

BART. (*Uneasy, in a much pleasanter tone than he's used so far.*) Now look, if I said anything out of line—

GLADYS. What do you call accusing her of being chummy with Harvey Spoonbill?

BART. A reporter has to investigate all possible leads—

ELLEN. Well, you can stop investigating right now, Mister Madden. Either you settle down for an interview like a decent journalist, or you're going through that door!

GLADYS. Whether the elevator's there or not.

BART. But—your P.R. gal made an appointment—

ELLEN. For an interview. And you'll have one. But first of all, turn that damned machine off! (*Reluctantly, he does so.*) That's better. Now, if you have a pad and pencil, perhaps we can do this in civilized manner.

BART. (*Removing sling-strap from neck.*) I have. I just hate to use them. My shorthand is really lousy.

GLADYS. At last! A sign of human frailty!

BART. (*Recorder and mike held uncertainly out toward her.*) Uh, where can I put these—?

GLADYS. Here, I'll put them away nice and careful.

(*Goes to table between armchairs, will set recorder and mike on its lower level, during:*) They'll be perfectly safe here, and you can pick them up when you go. Not one moment before!

ELLEN. Do you agree?

BART. (*Raises hand in Scout's Honor gesture.*) . . . I agree. (*Takes pad and pencil from pocket.*)

ELLEN. (*Now briskly polite and at ease.*) Fine. Now, let's begin with a tour of the premises. I'll go slowly so you can write down everything you see. (*Has started toward kitchen, BART reluctantly tailing after her.*) We'll start with the kitchen and terrace, and then the upstairs . . . (*Has turned on last line, slightly, for an eye-to-eye with GLADYS over BART's shoulder; GLADYS silently gives the "okay" sign with one hand, then points to self, to the stairs, and makes a shepherding gesture, indicating that she will bring the Navy down that way while ELLEN takes BART up the other.*)

GLADYS. If there's a strong east wind, Mister Madden, try the view from the parapet! (*ELLEN exits to kitchen; GLADYS immediately bolts up stairs and out of sight.*)

ELLEN. (*Off.*) Come along, Mister Madden. . . . (*BART dashes to recorder, turns it on, but leaves it where it is, then hurries off after her; a moment later, GLADYS—preceded by a smiling, still-reeling BILL, who carries a mug in one hand and a coffeepot in the other—comes down the stairs into the living room. She is carrying a boxed chess set, and over the next several lines she will place box atop table between armchairs, then move the table further upstage toward elevator door, then move the two armchairs up to face each other across the table, and begin to remove chessmen and board from box, and to set it up, properly, but nearly helterskelter in her haste.*)

GLADYS. Come on, sailor, keep drinking that coffee. I have a few arrangements to make, fast!

BILL. But I wanna talk to Rosie—!

GLADYS. Can't I get it through your head?! Her name is not "Rosie"! She is Ellen Latimer, the wife of your best friend, and that means hands off, even if you *are* on shore leave!

BILL. (*Absorbs this dimly, then ventures:*) But she *looks* like Rosie . . . ?

GLADYS. Well, she's not!

BILL. (*Each of his replies, till he is seated, are preceded by a short thoughtful pause as he thinks over her speeches.*) Then—then why did she call me Sam?

GLADYS. Who knows?! Maybe she thinks you *look* like a Sam! (*Pauses in her work to look suspiciously at him.*) You are Bill, aren't you—? Commander William Rutledge—?

BILL. Uh. Well, I am, on the *ship*, of course . . . but on shore leave—

GLADYS. Oh. I think I get the idea. But none of your shenanigans while you're a guest in this apartment, you understand? You are Bill, and Ellen is Ellen, got it?! Who *is* this Rosie, anyway?

BILL. (*Allows her to seat him with a thud in left armchair.*) Rosie O'Reilly. A garbage collector I used to know. Wonderful girl.

GLADYS. You think Ellen Latimer looks like a garbage collector?!

BILL. Of course not! On the other hand, neither did Rosie. (*Begins to ponder her activity.*) Say, what are you doing, anyway—?

GLADYS. I figured as long as you can hardly hold your head up or talk straight, a chessboard would make a good disguise. You can lean over it with your forehead on both your hands, and never say a word, and it won't look funny. It's not much of a plan, but I didn't have much time to think it up. There! (*Dusts off hands after setting last chessman in place.*) You start leaning, and I'll go see how your best friend is doing with that hot tamale in the maid's-room—! (*Has almost started that way, but stops as* DUNCAN *enters; his manner shows outward calm over inner agitation.*)

DUNCAN. Gladys! This is no time to play games!

GLADYS. The *empty* armchair is for *you,* oh man of many secrets. What did you do with *"Tico-Tico"*— tie her to the bed?

DUNCAN. Where would I get a *rope?!*

GLADYS. Then where is she? She was trailing you like a lovelorn puppy a few minutes ago.

DUNCAN. I told her we were playing a game, and she can't come out here till she counts to one hundred —in English!

GLADYS. *Then* what?

DUNCAN. (*Sinking into armchair opposite* BILL.) If my prayers are answered there'll be an earthquake and I can hide in the rubble.

ILONA. (*Pops into room to query:*) Duncan? Que viene después "treinta-nueve"?

DUNCAN. Forty!

ILONA. *Ah, si! Gracias!* (*Pops out.*)

BILL. What was she thanking you for?

DUNCAN. For telling her what comes after thirty-nine.

GLADYS. You should've said "twenty"!

DUNCAN. I'm saving that till she reaches ninety.

GLADYS. Duncan—listen—I have a *confession* to make . . .

BILL. That reporter's going to think he's found the Promised Land!

DUNCAN. Well, he's wrong. This is the Last Days of Pompeii! What confession, Gladys?

GLADYS. I eavesdropped on you and Bill. I know you met Ilona the day you married Ellen.

DUNCAN. No-no, Gladys! Can't you get anything right? I met *Ellen* the day I married *Ilona!*

GLADYS. *What?!* Duncan—you and that jolly jumping-bean are man and wife?!

DUNCAN. Keep your voice down, for pete's sake! Of course we're not!

GLADYS. Then you *didn't* marry her?

DUNCAN. Well, sort of, but—

GLADYS. Sort of?! How can you get sort-of married?

BILL. Well, they went through the ceremony all right—

DUNCAN. But Diego recovered from his amnesia—

BILL. So when Dunc went back to the cafe—

GLADYS. *Hold* it! *Who* Diego? *What* cafe? (*Straightens abruptly, head half-turning toward stairs.*) Oh-oh, better save it! I hear them coming! Start playing chess! (*Exits speedily to kitchen with mug and coffeepot, during:*)

BILL. I don't know *how* to play.

DUNCAN. You don't have to! Just bend over the board and do everything you see *me* doing.

BILL. Gotcha.

(DUNCAN *positions his chair nearer the board; so does* BILL; DUNCAN *runs nervous finger around inside collar; so does* BILL; DUNCAN *glances nervously toward stairs, then shakes his head in despair, shudders, presses his palms together—fingers pointing upward—and raises his eyes heavenward in silent supplication; then he notices that* BILL *has matched each movement a fractional second later, and is now—since his heavenward stare prevents him seeing that* DUNCAN *is now staring at him—holding that final pose.*)

DUNCAN. (*After an exasperated take.*) Not *everything*, you idiot! Just the moves of the chess game!

BILL. But you said—

DUNCAN. Oh, shut up, they're coming! (*Leans forward over board, forehead cradled against fingertips, elbows on table edge;* BILL *duplicates this, and an instant later* ELLEN, *with* BART *behind her, descends stairs into view; she stops uncertainly at floor level on seeing duo.*)

BART. (*Comes down beside her, also staring at duo; then:*) Did we come back to the right penthouse—?

ELLEN. What—? Oh, yes, certainly. Uh. This is my husband, Drunken Latimer— *Duncan* Latimer—! (*Without looking up,* DUNCAN *grunts.*) —and this is my—that is, *his*—very good friend— (*Realizing danger too late,* DUNCAN *straightens and opens mouth, but before he can speak,* ELLEN *has finished:*) —Sam Coleman. (BILL *now reacts too late, meets* DUNCAN's *unhappy gaze, then both men re-concentrate on chessboard;* ELLEN, *not sure what to do next, adds for want of something better:*) Sam is—a naval man.

BART. I'm a leg man, myself. (*Getting only a narrow-eyed grimace from* ELLEN *on this so-so display of wit, he leans over twosome and observes:*) Their concentration is amazing—especially when you consider neither man has moved a piece yet.

DUNCAN. (*Spurred by this observation, quickly makes a move;* BILL *instantly makes another;* DUNCAN *does the same; they go back and forth in this manner for at least a dozen lightning moves within about ten seconds' time, then go rigid with intensity and stare at the board for a long moment, as* ELLEN *and* BART *react with amazement at that blur of activity; then:*) Hmmm. Very interesting.

BART. It certainly is. Sam just captured his own king.

ELLEN. (*Reacts, then covers quickly with:*) This isn't regular chess.

DUNCAN. (*To* BART *in swift corroboration.*) Right! Sam and I are anti-war. We play a peaceful version. First man to capture his own king proclaims a democracy. (*All stare at* BILL, *awaiting his proclamation; he stares at them uncertainly, then abruptly hiccups;* DUNCAN *stands.*) Your game!

BART. That's a proclamation of democracy? A hiccup?

ELLEN. Well, nearly everybody drinks. (*Takes*

BART'S *arm to forestall further comment, starts tow-*
*ing him kitchenward, babbling in a single breath:*)
And that reminds me, I'm forgetting my manners,
wouldn't *you* like a drink, why of *course* you would,
*really* it's no trouble at all, *Gladys*, get a clean glass
for Mister Madden—! (*They are off, into kitchen,*
*and almost simultaneous with their disappearance we*
*hear from maid's-room:*)

ILONA. (*Off.*) *Wahn-hahndrad!* (*As a galvanized*
DUNCAN *rises to his feet, she rushes in with arms held*
*wide as if for a congratulatory embrace.*) *Esta todos!*
*Termino!* (*Before he can speak, she claps heels of her*
*hands to her temples, remembering something.*) *Ay!*
*Soy alocado! Que olvido! Yo tengo un don por te,*
*Duncan!* (*Rushes out again, leaving* DUNCAN *in stance*
*of man about to speak to her, mouth working, finger*
*half-pointing her way.*)

BILL. (*Almost sober now, thanks to pressure of*
*events.*) And what was all that about?

DUNCAN. (*Without turning.*) Which part?

BILL. (*Getting to his feet with hardly a wobble,*
*now.*) Suit yourself.

DUNCAN. She said she is stupid and forgetful and
has a gift for me.

BILL. (*Resting his knuckles on table, steadying him-*
*self bit by bit.*) What kind of gift?

DUNCAN. (*Faces him, on:*) Something ghastly.

BILL. She said that?

DUNCAN. No, I said that.

BILL. You can't be sure. It might be something nice.

DUNCAN. With *my* luck? (*Turns back toward* ILONA
*as she rushes in waving long garment.*)

ILONA. *He aqui!* (*Stops to flourish it, holding it by*
*shoulders, so that* DUNCAN *and we see it is a long*
*flannel nightshirt, bright red, on the breast of which*
*are an overlapping pair of large arrow-pierced hearts,*
*one monogrammed "D" and the other "I."*) *Por te,*
*mi novio, con todo mi corazon!*

BILL. (*As a wildly smiling* DUNCAN *grabs it from*

*her and scrunches it to his chest to hide the damning monogram.*) You don't have to translate that one. She just broke the language barrier.

DUNCAN. (*Smiling fiercely for* ILONA'S *benefit, but speaking through clenched teeth as he backs in terror and panic toward stairs.*) Good! Then talk to her! Say anything! Just keep her occupied for five minutes while I figure out how to get *rid* of this thing! (*To* ILONA, *while backing up stairs:*) Me gusta, querida! Esta muy bonita! Muchas gracias! (*Turns and bolts from sight, just as* GLADYS *gallops back into room from kitchen, arms waving wildly.*)

GLADYS. Positions, everybody, they're headed this way—! Oh, no! What's *she* doing here?! Bill, where's Duncan?!

BILL. If the upstairs medicine cabinet contains a bottle of iodine, he is drinking it. And don't call me *Bill!*

GLADYS. Oh, yeah, I forgot you used the Sam Coleman routine on Rosie.

BILL. Gladys! You *know* the Sam Coleman routine? *Know* about Rosie?

GLADYS. Of course I do!

BILL. But before, you said—

GLADYS. Naturally! I couldn't let on to *you* how much *I* knew till *I* knew how much *you* knew!

BILL. Then Dunc and his wife know all about each other—?!

GLADYS. Don't be ridiculous! As professional performers, they tell their *P.R. person everything;* as a typical husband and wife, they don't tell *each other anything!*

ILONA. *Que?*

GLADYS. Who the hell is Kay?!

BILL. That's Spanish. She wants to know what the hell is happening around here.

GLADYS. (*To* ILONA:) Join the club. (*To* BILL:) I

sure wish Duncan had seen fit to confide in me about *her,* the louse!

BILL. *Her* the louse?

GLADYS. No, *him* the louse, *her* the fly in the ointment! How the hell do I take the top mudslinger of Mystique Magazine coyly aside and explain Duncan's extra wife?! If there were only some way to distract him from her . . . (*At this moment, the nightshirt returns: It is outside and against the window, an out-of-view sleeve apparently snagged on a projection somewhere above our view when* DUNCAN *flung it out into space from the bedroom; the monogram is in full view; it is behind* GLADYS, *but* BILL *and* ILONA *react at once.*)

BILL. How about *that?* (*Points in a gesture as weak and weary as his voice.*)

ILONA. (*Babbles while* GLADYS *is turning to look.*) *Mi don! Por que esta mi don allá—?!*

GLADYS. Good gravy, what's that?! Do *you* know? No, wait, I don't *want* to know! But I've *got* to know! Hold it, I *do* know! The monogram is worth ten thousand words! (*Lurches toward pull-cord, and will draw drapes closed in a flash, as she finishes, despairingly:*) I should never have asked for a salary. I should've asked for mileage! (*Just as she finishes,* DUNCAN *trots debonairly down stairs into room again, reacts to tableau, stops at foot of stairs.*)

DUNCAN. (*Just as* ELLEN *and* BART, *each with a drink in hand, enter from kitchen, and pause just below table at his line:*) Gladys— Why did you draw those drapes—?!

GLADYS. It's cozier this way!

ILONA. *Yo no comprendo—que passe—?*

BART. (*Moving toward her.*) Ah, and whom have we here . . . ? (*Gets to her, takes her hands, then notices frozen silence on part of others, who all stand in immobile uncertainty.*) Isn't anybody going to introduce me?

OTHERS. *No!* (*He reacts, and all realize this won't do, so all instantly—and variously—try to make sense by saying something like:*) That is to say— What we meant was— You see, Mister Madden— I mean— (*This is said in unison, all phrases overlapping, then all come to a lame halt after this chaos of sound.*)

ILONA. *Que dice—?*

BART. Ah, she's Spanish! *Habla Ingles?*

ILONA. *No. Habla Espanol?*

BART. Oh, *si, senorita!*

DUNCAN. Oh, no!

BART. What's the matter?

DUNCAN. Nothing! I mean—no, she's not a senorita —she's a senora!

ILONA. *Si-si, soy senora!*

BART. Oh, I see.

ILONA. *Si?*

BART. No-no. *"Comprendo."*

ILONA. *No comprendo?*

GLADYS. Hold it! Not another word till we get an interpreter!

BART. I'm sorry. I was just trying to find out who the young lady is.

ELLEN. She's our new cook.

BART. Oh, really?

ELLEN. Why should I *lie* about it?

DUNCAN. (*As if backing up his wife, but actually trying to get rid of* ILONA, *points dramatically toward the kitchen, on:*) Ilona, make the man a taco!

ILONA. (*Points uncertainly at* BART.) *Eso hombre—?*

GLADYS. (*To* BART.) Congratulations, you're a taco!

BART. Wait a minute—it's the strangest thing—she looks familiar— (*Suddenly snaps fingers.*) The painting! Of course! That's where I saw that face!

DUNCAN. Nonsense!

BILL. You're imagining things.

BART. I couldn't be mistaken! But . . . (*Turns to* ELLEN.) Why in the world would you have a portrait of your *cook* on the wall?

GLADYS. (*As* ELLEN *flounders for a reply.*) It was cheaper than raising her pay.

BART. Raising her pay? I thought she was a *new* cook.

ELLEN. She is, but she's very greedy.

BILL. Still, good cooks are hard to get—

GLADYS. So we gave in to her demands!

DUNCAN. (*Without thinking, places arm across* ILONA'S *shoulders.*) After all, you know how hard it is to hold a good servant . . . (*Realizes this is unfortunate, yanks arm away, blurts:*) I mean, keep a woman . . . (*This is worse; tries again.*) Uh. Did you ever need *help?*

GLADYS. Not as bad as you do.

DUNCAN. (*Abruptly steps to* BILL, *changes topic.*) Say, old buddy, how about another game?!

BART. How can you see the board in this twilight zone?

ELLEN. Yes, why is it so dark in here?

GLADYS. (*Points at chessboard, inspired.*) Night maneuvers!

ILONA. (*Moves to take* DUNCAN'S *arm.*) *Que passe, Duncan? Yo no tiendo—*

BART. (*To* ELLEN.) She calls him by his first name?

ELLEN. It was in her contract. Right, Dunc?

BART. (*To* DUNCAN.) Isn't she sure?

DUNCAN. (*Before he can think it through.*) Well, she doesn't know any Spanish.

BART. (*To* ELLEN.) Then how do you communicate with her?

BILL. I gave her a Spanish cookbook.

ELLEN. I thought that was from Bill Rutledge . . . ?

BILL. Uh.

DUNCAN. She just misunderstood me in the dark! Here, let's clear things up—! (*Goes to drape-cord, but before he can pull it:*)

BILL and GLADYS. *No, don't!* (*As he freezes, startled:*)

GLADYS. The track is jammed!

BILL. Right! You could've pulled the whole fixture down on your head!

BART. Excuse me, but— Who is Bill Rutledge?

DUNCAN. (*Desperate.*) First things first! Let me fix that jammed curtain! (*Makes it sound vicious as "damned curtain."*)

GLADYS. Uh—

BILL. Dunc—

DUNCAN. (*Now at overlap of drapes in center of window.*) Sometimes it snags at the overlap. If you tug at the carrier just so— (*Has taken left and right sections of drape-edge in left and right hand, moving them just far apart enough so that he alone will be able to see through the window beyond them.*) —it often pops right out, and— (*Sees.*) Aaaaagh! (*Drops drapes, spins about, flattens himself back against overlap, arms out at shoulder height, palms backward against drapes, a grin of idiotic fear on his face.*) Sorry to scream. Strained a muscle. That thing is really stuck.

BILL. Sure is!

GLADYS. You better believe it!

ELLEN. It's never stuck that badly before . . . ?

BILL. *Oh*, yes it has!

DUNCAN. We didn't have the heart to tell you.

GLADYS. You've been so busy.

BILL. Carrying all that garbage. (*Winces, too late.*)

BART. Garbage?

GLADYS. He means supporting all her sponsors' products!

ELLEN. They never give me a moment's rest!

DUNCAN. Rest! That reminds me—! (*Grabs* ILONA's *elbow, starts rushing her off, right.*) Have you forgotten, dear girl? It's almost past your *nap* time!

BART. (*One beat after they have vanished.*) . . . "Nap time"?!

GLADYS. It was part of her contract.

ELLEN. Her picture on the wall—

BILL. And the original in her cozy little bed—

GLADYS. Every afternoon, like clockwork.

BART. She must be one hell of a cook.

BILL. You should taste her kolachkes.

ELLEN. (*As* BART *reacts, but before he can quite comment.*) Listen, let's get on with that interview, shall we? Gladys and Sam can—uh—play chess, or something . . . ?

GLADYS. (*As she and* BILL *instantly sit down to chessboard.*) Great idea! There's nothing I like more than creating new democracies! (BILL *hiccups.*) Would you mind waiting till I get the pieces on the board?

BILL. I like to take my opponents by surprise. (*Both start to ineptly set up board, while a curious* BART *moves slowly closer, puzzled at their ineptitude.*)

ELLEN. (*Sensing disaster, drains her drink, sets glass on table.*) Hey! Let's get going, Mister Madden. Why don't we go out on the terrace, and—

BART. Won't that be kind of chilly?

ELLEN. I thought our chitchat might disturb their game.

GLADYS. Oh, not at all. Besides, as your P.R. person, I should have firsthand knowledge about anything you're going to get in print.

BART. Well, that's fine by me—though it is a little dark in here to take notes.

ELLEN. (*Before* BILL *or* GLADYS *realize her intent, starts for cord.*) Here, maybe *I* can get this thing unjammed. I'm sure if I tug it just the right way—

BILL. (*As he and* GLADYS *come frantically to their feet, blurts:*) Rosie—!

BART. (*Moves toward them as* GLADYS *tries to look innocently ceilingward and just as* ELLEN—*turning a startled look back toward* BILL—*automatically opens the drapes, on:*) What did he say—? (*Then he and* BILL *see what the two women have not seen:* DUNCAN *is inching along the ledge, his face toward the*

*room, but his eyes covered by his right hand in fear; his
other arm is spread-eagled to the side, palms and
fingers flat on the pane, as he gropes for the dangling
nightshirt—which has now flipped over so we can
see what it is, but not see the hearts or monograms.*)

BILL. (*Improvising wildly but without conviction.*)
Rosy! The nightshirt! The color! . . . Isn't it—
rosy . . . ?!

ELLEN. (*As she and* GLADYS *both turn for a look.*)
What nightshirt—? (*Then both react to the sight of*
DUNCAN's *location.*) Dunc!

GLADYS. (*Rushes to her before she can topple backward, supports her.*) Don't scream! He'll hear you!

ELLEN. But he'll be killed!

BILL. He'll be fine as long as you don't excite him!

BART. (*Moving with others toward window.*) But
why is he out there?

GLADYS. To get that nightshirt, of course!

ELLEN. But why is that nightshirt out there?

BILL. Well, you wouldn't want a thing like that in
here.

GLADYS. Will you all shut up! If he hears us and
opens his eyes, he might fall!

BART. She's right! Nobody make a sound!

ELLEN. Oh, Dunc! Dunc!

GLADYS. Ssh!

ELLEN. But—

OTHERS. *Sssssh!*

BILL. (*After they watch his fearful progress a moment, whispers:*) What if he opens his eyes and sees
us?

GLADYS. (*Whispers.*) You're right! That could scare
him, too!

BART. (*Whispers.*) Maybe somebody should close
the drapes. (*Nobody moves.*)

ELLEN. Good idea. (*Nobody moves.*)

GLADYS. Any volunteers?

OTHERS. *Sssssh!* (BART *goes to take sip of his drink*

*but* GLADYS *grabs it from him, but before she can sip,* ELLEN *notices, takes it from her, but* BILL *notices, grabs the glass.*)

BILL. My turn! (*Takes glass, drains drink, sets glass on magazine table with a loud clunking sound; others ad-lib shushes at him.*) Sorry.

ILONA. (*Comes rushing in, and up to group, which is now convened in a sidewalk-superintendent semi-circle below magazine table, observing* DUNCAN'S *steady edging nightshirtward.*) *Ai-ai-ai! Duncan esta fuera mi ventana!*

BART. She says Duncan is out her window.

ILONA. (*Tugging* BART'S *arm as she flails finger toward maid's-room.*) *El sera muerte!*

BART. She says he will become dead.

GLADYS. Will you two stop playing *Sesame Street?!*

ELLEN. Quiet, all of you! You'll startle him! (*At this moment,* DUNCAN *reaches garment, turns his head and uncovers his eyes to see if he's reached his goal, smiles in relief and pulls nightshirt free of snag, then turns face back toward room, eyes open, and reacts to sight of his audience by gaping and almost toppling backward; others all scream and face downstage instantly, covering faces; on ledge,* DUNCAN *recovers, blows out his breath in a sigh of shaky relief, then edges gingerly but quickly back to his right and out of sight again, during:*)

ILONA. *No puedo mirar! No puedo mirar!*

BART. She can't look. She can't look.

GLADYS. (*Uncovers face to glare at him.*) Now cut that out!

BILL. (*As others uncover faces but do not turn toward window.*) Isn't *anybody* going to look?

ELLEN. I can't! I just can't! Sam—please—*you* look! Nothing bothers you!

BILL. (*Uncovers own face.*) All right. I'll do it! (*Abruptly turns, sees now-vacant ledge.*) Oh, no!

ELLEN. What is it?!

BILL. Don't look! (*All instantly turn and look, adlib things like "Oh, no!" and "Dunc!" and "Ai-ai-ai!" and rush around low table to get near enough to stand on tiptoe and look down out window.*)

ELLEN. My darling!

BILL. My buddy!

GLADYS. My ten percent!

ELLEN. (*As a shaky* DUNCAN *emerges from maid's-room corridor, trailing the nightshirt along the floor from one hand, and makes his weary way up behind group members as they jockey for position to see out window into the street below.*) Oh, Dunc! Oh, my darling! Where is he? I don't see him! (*Turns head to* GLADYS, *beside her.*) Why did he do it? Why was he out there? (*Sensing a presence, turns to face* DUNCAN, *now behind her.*) What in the world was he thinking of—?! (*Gasps in abrupt recognition.*) *Dunc!*

DUNCAN. (*Waves weakly.*) Hi, there!

ELLEN. (*Rushes and embraces him as others come away from window.*) Oh, you're alive, you're alive! (*Relief abruptly turns to reaction-anger and she pulls back from him furiously.*) What the hell were you *doing* out there, you muttonhead?!

DUNCAN. (*Pointing upstairs, at window, etc., tries futilely:*) The nightshirt—uh—see, the bedroom window was open—it must have fallen out or something—well, when I saw it—I mean—well, you *know* how tough New York is about *littering*—! (*Abruptly gives up, turns and starts toward kitchen.*) I need a drink!

GLADYS. (*Takes his arm and stops him.*) *I'll* get it! You sit down before you *faint!* (*There is just the hint of a hint in her inflection.*)

DUNCAN. (*Missing hint.*) Gladys, I've never fainted in my life!

BART. Mister Latimer, I have a question about that nightshirt—

DUNCAN. (*Suddenly lurching toward armchair.*) You know, I *do* feel faint!

BART. Now, just a minute—!

DUNCAN. Ooooooh! (*"Faints" into armchair.*)

ELLEN. (*Rushing to his side.*) *Now* see what you've done! (*Pulls nightshirt from* DUNCAN'S *hand, waves it in* BART'S *face.*) Why must you persecute him for your stupid story, just because of this ridiculous . . . (*Looks more closely at what she holds.*) . . . nightshirt . . . (*Spreads it wide, looks intently at monogram, then looks narrow-eyed toward* ILONA.) . . . *What* did you say your name was—?

ILONA. (*Smiling blankly.*) *Que?*

GLADYS. (*Quickly.*) See? Her name is "Kay"! Now, here, let me put that nightshirt up in Duncan's bureau drawer—!

BART. That's not her name. That's Spanish for "what"!

GLADYS. Don't ask *me* for what! *I* don't speak Spanish! Now, if you'll give *me* that nightshirt—

ELLEN. Wait just a minute! I want to know who gave *Dunc* this nightshirt!

BILL and GLADYS. *I* did! (*As they give each other a look of helpless exasperation:*)

BART. *Both* of you—?

BILL. It was very expensive—

GLADYS. The monogram and all—

BILL. So we split the cost.

BART. And just what is the *meaning* of the monogram—?!

GLADYS. (*Opens mouth, hesitates, then says to* BILL:) *Tell* him, Sam!

BILL. (*Trapped, at first gapes, then is suddenly inspired.*) It's his old *Navy* nightshirt! He used to be a *drill instructor!* (*Indicating letters.*) "D"—"I"! Drill Instructor!

ELLEN. And the hearts with the arrow through them—?!

GLADYS. (*What the hell, anything's worth a try:*) He loved his work!

DUNCAN. (*Suddenly surges to his feet, grabs night-*

*shirt, starts for stairs, on:*) Excuse me, I'll be right back!

ELLEN. Dunc, where are you going?!

DUNCAN. (*Pauses with dramatic dignity at foot of stairs.*) This morning I had four cups of coffee, heaven knows how many double scotches, and considering what I nearly had scared out of me on that window ledge, you should be able to *guess!* (*Turns and bolts up stairs out of sight.*)

ELLEN. (*Rushes to foot of stairs to shout up after him.*) Duncan Latimer, if you expect me to believe—! (*Suddenly pauses, looks uneasily toward* BART; *her normal caution in his presence vanished during* DUNCAN'S *peril on the ledge, but it is all at once back in full force; she smiles, suddenly, and trills a high, giddy, hollow laugh, in which* GLADYS, *then* BILL, *and even a bewildered* ILONA *join; then* ILONA *shrugs and stops, and* ELLEN *says lightly:*) Oh, well, you know how temperamental artists are! Shall we get on with our interview—?

BART. Just a moment. There seems to be a discrepancy here— If that's Mister Latimer's old *Navy* nightshirt, how come *Sam* and *Gladys* bought it for him?

GLADYS. Nothing's too good for our boys overseas!

ELLEN. Of course not! Mister Madden, you have a terribly suspicious mind. Why, Duncan Latimer is one of the most loving and trustworthy men I've ever known in my life!

BART. Then why did you imply there was something between him and this woman? (*Points to* ILONA.)

ELLEN. I didn't mean *that* woman. I meant *this* woman! (*Points to* GLADYS.)

GLADYS. *What?!* Honestly, Ellen, I hardly even *shake hands* with him!

BILL. Then how does he know you're ticklish?

ELLEN. Oh, for heaven's sake, I didn't mean anything like *that!* I just meant that you, as our P.R.

representative, know everything about us, so you undoubtedly knew about his Navy nightshirt, and I resented the fact that you never told me what a sentimental fool he was! (*Folds her arms in triumph, says to* BART:) Now go make a juicy scandal out of that!

GLADYS. Don't tempt him, he may do it! (*As if reading imaginary headline:*) "What Mystery Woman Knew More Than Duncan's Wife about His Navy Nightshirt?"

BART. Hey, thanks! That's a beauty!

BILL. (*Dryly.*) Nice going, Gladys!

BART. Look, we can argue that part later. I have to get some details straight. (*To* ILONA.) *Donde esta que tu duermes?*

ILONA. (*Gesturing.*) *Dentro la camara de la doncella.*

BART. (*To* GLADYS *and* BILL.) Well, if she sleeps in the maid's-room, where do you two sleep?

GLADYS *and* BILL. (*With a simultaneous gesture, each thinking only of self.*) On the sofa. (*Both react to unexpected response of other with winces.*)

ELLEN. (*Quickly.*) But not at the same time!

BILL. (*Picking up the ball.*) We sleep in shifts!

GLADYS. (*Missing implication of her line till it's spoken.*) The sofa's too small for both of us at once— (*Realizes implication, adds lamely:*) —I *imagine!*

BART. (*Busily scribbling in his notebook.*) Yes-yes. Uh—Commander—where are you stationed?

BILL. Huh? Oh. I'm on the U.S.S. Petoskey. That is —when I'm *on* it, I'm on the Petoskey.

BART. (*Murmuring what he is transcribing onto the page.*) . . . Coleman . . . Sam . . . Commander . . . Petoskey . . .

BILL. (*Very uneasy now.*) Uh—excuse me, Mister Madden—you—don't intend to *print* any of this—?

BART. Is there some reason I shouldn't?

BILL. (*Floundering.*) Uh. Well. No. Only. It's just that—

GLADYS. (*To the rescue.*) The interview is about *Ellen*. Your readers want to know about *her*. Why drag in a lot of extraneous characters?!

ELLEN. Sam—I understand *perfectly* why you *don't* want to be in the *article*—but (*Sotto voce.*) —why *don't* you want to be in the article?! (*It is completely clear to both audience and others onstage that she is torn between her professional reputation being at stake and the fact that, as a woman, she is dying of suspicious curiosity about his hesitancy; it is also clear to her, and she wilts wearily as others stare at her.*)

BILL. (*Out of exasperation and also a vestige of gallantry.*) Who in their right mind wants to be written up in Mystique Magazine!

BART. As Mystique Magazine's top writer, I resent that!

BILL. Well, you go right ahead! (*Starts toward kitchen.*) Meantime, as long as nobody seems ready to offer me some lunch, I am declaring martial law and fully intend to ravish your refrigerator! (*Stops as* ELLEN *grabs his arm.*)

ELLEN. Sam, wait! Don't be mad! I can explain everything!

BART. Explain? What do you have to explain? Why should Ellen Latimer be so concerned about Sam Coleman? (*Looks hard at* BILL, *who guppy-mouths ineffectually; then at* ELLEN, *who does the same; then at* GLADYS, *who starts to do same, then considers, then shrugs, then says:*)

GLADYS. He once took this thorn out of her paw . . .

ELLEN. (*Even as* BART *is about to question* GLADYS *further, grabs his arm and propels him toward kitchen.*) Hasn't she got a delightful sense of humor! Ah-ha-ha! But I'm being a terrible hostess, I forgot about your drink, the one Sam drank instead of you, let me make you another, shall we, you do drink, don't you—? Ah-ha-ha! *C'mon!* (*On last phrase, literally jerks him offstage into kitchen.*)

BILL. (*As he and* GLADYS *converge near front of elevator.*) Gladys, listen, we've got to—to— (*Stops suddenly, suspiciously, looking at* ILONA, *who stands smiling sweetly and blankly at the two of them.*) Uh, young lady, are you sure that—uh—that is—do you speak *any* English—?

ILONA. *Que?*

GLADYS. (*Inspired.*) Wait, there's just a chance that— (*To* ILONA:) *Parlez-vous français?*

ILONA. (*Brightly.*) *O! Oui! Je parle un peu de français!*

GLADYS. (*With rising hope.*) *Sprechen-Sie Deutsch?*

ILONA. (*Even more brightly.*) *Ach, ja! Ich spreche eine kleine Deutsch!*

GLADYS. (*Hardly realizing the mishmash of her statement, which is made admirably clear with accompanying gestures:*) *Bueno!* Then please *gehen-Sie* the hell out of this *zimmer* so Sam *et moi* can *parlons* in private, *versteh?* C'mon! *Andale! Vite! Schnell! Fa via!* (*Her wildly waving arms and gestures toward maid's-room have their effect, and a wide-eyed* ILONA *flees off to shelter.*)

BILL. (*Quietly, as* GLADYS *catches her breath in relief.*) You know, you could make a bundle at the U.N. What did you tell her, anyway?

GLADYS. Who knows?! The main thing is, she got the message! Now come on, let's formulate some plan of action before the enemy returns!

BILL. Anything less than murder wouldn't be fool-proof.

GLADYS. I know. Isn't it ghastly?! So help me, if one more thing goes wrong, I am going to crawl underneath that table and hold my breath until I die! (*At this point, the nightshirt reappears outside the window, the same sleeve caught on the same snag;* BOTH *sense the motion, turn and look, shut their eyes and shake their heads, and then* GLADYS *quietly gets*

*on hands and knees and crawls underneath the dinette
table;* BILL *watches, exasperated, then calmly moves
toward pull-cord of drapes.*)

BILL. Don't be such a defeatist. We closed these
things once, we can close them again . . . ? (*His inflection changes as he realizes he cannot find pull-cord,
and he has just started back behind drapes to locate it,
on following line*—) Where the hell did that cord get
to—?! (—*when* ILONA *emerges timidly from right corridor, looks about, sees no one, and then less timidly
strolls toward chess table; at this point,* BART *re-enters
from kitchen, moving furtively and fast, and rushes
right to get recorder and turn it off, meantime calling
back over his shoulder.*)

BART. Take your time with the drinks, I'm in no
hurry. Then we'll have our little chat—! (GLADYS *has
reacted with embarrassed stupefaction at her own
location, and shifts back a bit so she won't be seen
and have to explain what she's doing there;* BILL, *unnoticed by* BART *or* ILONA, *has poked his head out from
behind drapes at the sound of* BART'S *voice, and almost speaks—but then both he and she react to the
fact that the recorder has been on, all this time—and
on* ILONA'S *line, neither would speak a sound for a
million dollars.*) There's more to this setup than meets
the eye. And I think I may have a few of the answers
right here on magnetic tape.

ILONA. (*With barely a trace of a Spanish accent:*)
I don't *like* this business, Bart! When you brought
me over here today, you said—

BART. We've been all over that! A deal is a deal!
I get what I want, and you get what you want!

ILONA. You *know* I'd never have agreed if you'd
told me Duncan had a *wife!* Fun is fun, but I never
figured on messing up his *marriage!*

BART. (*During business of removing cassette, flip-
ping it over, and re-inserting it into recorder.*) Don't
forget you signed a contract with us. All I have to

do is show it to the immigration authorities, and you'll
be deported as an undesirable alien. Then just *try* to
get U.S. citizenship!

ILONA. Oooh! *Que hombre servil, tu sucio cochinillo,
hijo de una perra—!!!*

BART. I'm glad I don't have to translate *that!*
(*Starts for telephone, carrying recorder.*) You know
the plan. Stick to it, or you can wave 'bye-'bye to the
land of the free! (*He glances warily kitchenward, then
picks up phone and starts to dial; ILONA quivers with
impotent fury, then angrily turns on her heel and
stalks off toward maid's-room, as BART gets his party
on phone and speaks covertly and quickly.*) Bart
Madden here. Not much time, so listen: Find out
everything you can about an officer named Sam Coleman, assigned to the U.S.S. Petoskey, and another
naval man—probably an officer, too—named Bill Rutledge, and call me right back. . . . At the Latimers',
right! . . . Oh, and see if you can dig up anything
about the name "Rosie" in connection with Ellen
Latimer, got it? . . . Oops, gotta go! (*Hangs up
swiftly as ELLEN enters from kitchen with a pair of
drinks; as she locates him, and hands him his drink,
DUNCAN comes trotting amiably downstairs, sees
them, and is going to speak, then glances right and
sees nightshirt, reacts, and swiftly—since they haven't
seen him yet—sidles to drapes and reaches behind
them for pull-cord; he reacts in shocked silence to
what he feels back there, turns his head wide-eyed,
and BILL—who has been pulling back from view and
re-emerging as circumstances dictated during the
BART-ILONA colloquy—sidles out into view, gives
DUNCAN a hapless smile, then with his still-hidden
hand pulls the drapes shut over the view of the
nightshirt; this catches the attention of ELLEN and
BART, who will turn in reaction at the (\*) below; however, they have been chatting, as follows, from*

ELLEN's *entrance through* DUNCAN's *entrance and*
BILL's *appearance from behind the drapes:*)

ELLEN. Oh, there you are. I hope this isn't too
strong. I'm not a very reliable bartender.

BART. The very fact that I'm accepting it at all
shows my confidence in your reliability. You'd be
surprised how many interviewees wouldn't draw the
line at attempting to *poison* me! (*He laughs at his
jest;* ELLEN, *to whom the notion did not occur till
then, reluctantly and unconvincingly joins him in
the laugh; then he looks at her a bit uncertainly, and
both their laughters trail off to nothing; he looks into
his glass, then at her face; recognizing his feelings,
she gives him a steely-eyed "Now,* really!" *glare,
and takes his glass from him, giving him her own in
return, taking a large swallow from his drink, then
staring accusingly at him.*) Well—a man can't be too
careful— (*Raises her drink toast-like but before he
can take a sip:* (\*), *and* BOTH *stare across the room
uncertainly at* DUNCAN *and* BILL.)

DUNCAN. (*Defensively, as* BILL *finishes drawing
drapes and stands there.*) It's cozier this way!

BART. (*Because of* GLADYS's *identical earlier line:*)
. . . Have we had this conversation before—? (*Sets
drink on cocktail table.*)

DUNCAN. (*In no mood for light badinage.*) The
light hurts my eyes! Believe it or not, take it or leave
it, suit yourself! Okay?!

BART. I only meant—

DUNCAN. Who the hell cares?!

ELLEN. (*As he strides stormily past them toward
kitchen.*) Dunc—?!

DUNCAN. I don't say another word until I get a
drink! And then, maybe, I am going to say *plenty!*
(*Exits to kitchen.*)

BART. (*To* ELLEN:) Is he always like this around
the house?

ELLEN. Oh, shut up! . . . *Dunc—!* (*Rushes off to*

*kitchen, too;* BART, *blinking at the abrupt vehemence, but also smiling with delight, turns to* BILL.)

BILL. (*Quietly, before* BART *can speak:*) *I* don't like you, either.

BART. You don't know how happy that makes me. If everybody's warm and friendly, I don't feel I'm getting down to the nitty-gritty! (*Turns and strolls off into kitchen, taking recorder;* BILL *instantly rushes to table, helping out* GLADYS, *who just as instantly has started scurrying forth.*)

BILL. The man's insidious! We've got to stop him! If he plays back all the stuff we've been blabbing near that recorder—!

GLADYS. (*Almost ignoring him as she rushes to press elevator button.*) Never mind the recorder! I've got a plan!

BILL. Never *mind—?!* Gladys, we've got to *get* that thing, destroy the *tape—!*

GLADYS. No-no, don't you see? That's the worst possible thing we could do! If we grab his tape, he'll know there are dangerous secrets here, and he'll *never* stop till he ferrets them out!

BILL. But if we *don't* grab the tape, he'll *play* it, and then he'll *know* all the secrets!

GLADYS. (*With a peculiar smile.*) Unh-uh. Not all. There are still *dozens* more secrets he hasn't learned.

BILL. Dozens?! Good grief! I had no idea—!

GLADYS. Listen, I don't have time to explain, now, I've got to get down to the lobby and talk to Marge!

BILL. Why don't you just use the phone—?

GLADYS. Because he might come back any minute and *hear* me—! (*BELL; she yanks door open, starts into elevator.*) Now *your* job, the instant I get back, is to take Bart Madden off someplace by yourself, so I can talk to Ellen and Duncan alone!

BILL. What? How? What can I tell him to lure him away?

GLADYS. Take him to the men's room and show him your obscene tattoo!

BILL. (*Reacts with indignation.*) What makes you think I have an obscene tattoo?

GLADYS. *All* Navy men have obscene tattoos!

BILL. (*After a pause.*) . . . It's not *that* obscene. . . !

GLADYS. Good! I knew you wouldn't let me down! And don't tell *anyone* I've gone!

BILL. But they'll see you come back—!

GLADYS. No they won't. I know the people in the apartment below here. I'll take the elevator to their floor and come up the rest of the way on the fire escape!

BILL. Won't the people downstairs think it's a little odd when you exit out their window?

GLADYS. I doubt it. They *know* I'm in show business . . . ! (*Exits, shutting door; a moment later, DUNCAN storms back in, now carrying a drink, from which he will sip shortly and viciously from time to time, plunks himself down at one end of the sofa as ELLEN and BART re-enter.*)

DUNCAN. Okay, let's get this damned invasion of privacy over with! All souls bared, no holds barred!

BART. (*Happily plunking himself down beside him.*) Now that's the kind of cooperation I like! Ellen, why don't you sit here beside us and we'll wind the whole thing up in no time!

ELLEN. (*Sitting gingerly at BART's other side.*) All right. I guess. Dunc . . . why don't you hold off drinking until we're through—? I—I wouldn't want you to say the wrong—that is, *pronounce* things incorrectly. You know how drinking makes you slur your words . . .

BART. Ah! Is that a fact! I didn't know that!

DUNCAN. Thanks a lot, Ellen!

ELLEN. I only meant—

BART. Now-now, don't squabble, please. Not till I

turn the machine on. (*Turns it on, sets it on cocktail table, then holds microphone to* ELLEN, *then to* DUNCAN, *seeking a volunteer.*) Now then—you were saying—? (*The sight of the microphone has dashed cold water over both moods, her unhappiness and his belligerence; they straighten a bit, knowing what they say now is "for the record"; then:*)

DUNCAN. (*Suddenly suave and smiling.*) Ellen, darling, this is *your* interview, after all, why don't *you* talk first?

ELLEN. (*Just as falsely sweet and serene.*) Why thank you, Duncan, my dearest one! What exactly was it that you wished to know, Mister Madden? About our perfect marriage—?

DUNCAN. Or our fabulously successful careers—?

ELLEN. Or the marvelous way we pursue both marriage and careers so flawlessly well—?

DUNCAN. (*Not noticing* ILONA *entering and standing watching him.*) Yes, what shall it be? Our incredible talents? Our undying devotion? Or just all the endless days of fantastic incomes and perfect hap— (*Now he notices, and gulps between syllables.*) —iness?

BART. (*As if not noticing* ILONA, *inquires as if lightly:*) Is anything wrong?

ELLEN and DUNCAN. (*In perfect sparkling unison.*) Nonsense!

DUNCAN. (*Beat.*) Of course not!

ELLEN. (*Beat.*) What a silly question! (*Both laugh airily in unison, and stop at same time, their smiles in place, but the rest of their expressions looking a bit less than carefree.*)

BART. (*As if now noticing, announces metrically:*) Ah, *look!* Here comes your *cook!*

BILL. I couldn't eat a thing.

DUNCAN. Come on, let's get this stupid interview over with, and then I've got to practice for tonight's concert!

ELLEN. And I have a million things to pack!

BART. Pack? Are you—going someplace, Mrs. Latimer—?

DUNCAN. No, she is *not* going someplace, *we* are going someplace, so get that stop-the-presses gleam out of your eye!

ILONA. (*In her pretty and pseudo-bewildered way, has now come across almost to cocktail table, beyond which* DUNCAN *is—in quietly controlled panic—patently ignoring her.*) Duncan . . . ?

DUNCAN. Not *now*, for the love of Pete!

ILONA. *Que?*

DUNCAN. *No ahora, por el amor de Pedro!*

BART. (*Turns microphone to* DUNCAN:) Say, that burst of Spanish reminds me: Tell me about that portrait. Isn't that an original Valdez?

DUNCAN. Portrait? What portrait? Oh, *that* portrait! Uh—why—yes it is. I—I had no idea you were such a student of the arts. . . .

BART. Oh, I'm not. But I spotted his signature in the lower right corner. Unless—it's not a *copy*, is it—?

ELLEN. (*Falling into the trap.*) Copy?! Of course not! We'd never have anything but an original!

BART. Ah! Then I *am* intrigued! "The reason I was intrigued is that a bit earlier, before the interview began, I had been informed that the woman in the painting is now the Latimer's new Spanish cook." Tell me, Mrs. Latimer—how did you arrange *that?*

ELLEN. I—I don't understand—

BART. I simply wondered whether you had Diego Valdez come over *here,* or if you shipped your cook over *there—?!*

ELLEN. Over *where?*

BART. (*Innocently.*) Why, to *Valencia,* of course . . . !

ELLEN. *Valencia?!* Dunc, you didn't tell me she came from Valencia—!

BART. Is there some significance in that particular location?

DUNCAN. Well—uh—just by the *craziest* coincidence —ha ha— (*His laugh is hollow and unconvincing.*) —that happens to be where I first met Ellen—

BART. Is that a fact!

ELLEN. Of course it's a fact! Why *shouldn't* we have met there?!

BART. I was just fascinated by the various coincidences—

DUNCAN. What coincidences?

BART. You meet in Valencia . . . Your cook is from Valencia . . . The painter of the portrait on your wall is from Valencia. . . .

DUNCAN. (*Very riled.*) Oh, don't stop *there!* If you want, I'll trot over to the piano and *play* "Valencia"! So what?!

ELLEN. (*Just as riled.*) I'm surprised you didn't make anything of the fact that we're just about to leave for *San Juan,* while you're at it! *Some* people like *rock and roll—we* favor *espanol!*

BART. Why are you talking in rhyme?

DUNCAN. Now, listen, you lay off her! What in hell is the matter with somebody having a *mad passion* for everything *Spanish—?!* (*He has come to his feet on the line, and of course it is the moment when* ILONA, *smiling torridly, her arms flung wide, tries to embrace him.*)

ILONA. *Duncan—!*

DUNCAN. (*Sits, instantly, trying to be too tiny to be seen.*) *Almost* everything!

ILONA. (*Will come around table and pull him gently to his feet, on:*) Ah, Duncan! Yo estoy aqui todo esa tiempe, y tu no toco nuestra cancion!

BART. (*As* ELLEN *narrows her eyes, and* DUNCAN *wilts:*) What does she mean, "I am here all this time, and you do not play our song!"?

ELLEN. (*Comes to her feet.*) *Their song?!*

DUNCAN. (*Babbling as* ILONA *tows him resolutely toward piano.*) Not "our song," hers and mine—she means "our song," hers and the other cooks in the

Spanish Culinary Union! . . . They play it at pep rallies!

ELLEN. *Duncan Latimer—!*

ILONA. (*Depositing a despairing* DUNCAN *onto piano bench.*) *Nuestra cancion, Duncan! Por favor!*

DUNCAN. (*All is lost, anyway, so—*) Oh, why the hell *not!* (*He begins to play the "Mexican Hat Dance" and* ILONA *begins to dance to it, just behind him, ad-libbing "Ole!" at each handclap-repeat, and* ELLEN *stands rigid with arms at her sides like ram-rods, and a smiling* BART *extends the microphone toward the music and singing; this is the tintinabulous tableau into which* GLADYS *walks—coming from the maid's-room; she stops aghast just inside room;* BILL *—who has been standing as a sort of world-weary observer of all goings-on since his last line, helpless to prevent the doom descending on his friend—sees her, after a moment, and immediately springs into action; he rushes to a startled* BART, *tugs him bodily to his feet, and—microphone and recorder going with them—practically drags him backward toward the stairs, on:*)

BART. (*Shouting over music and* ILONA'S *sporadic cries.*) Hey! What the hell are you doing? Let go of me!

BILL. (*Shouting for same reason.*) Not until you've seen my obscene tattoo! (*And as a dazed, robot-like* DUNCAN *continues to play, an effervescent* ILONA *continues to dance, a dumbfounded* GLADYS *continues to stare, a furious* ELLEN *continues to glare, and a determined* BILL *drags a startled* BART *toward the stairs—*)

## *THE CURTAIN FALLS*

## ACT THREE

*As curtain rises, it is just a few seconds later; BILL and BART are gone, but others are as we left them; DUNCAN plays "Mexican Hat Dance" through the first three handclap-Ole! combinations, but as he arrives at the spot for the fourth, and before ILONA can clap or shout her one-word lyric:*

GLADYS. (*Flings arms up and out for attention, and exclaims, in tempo and in place of the "Ole!":*) Okay! (*It is loud enough that ILONA stops on one foot, DUNCAN stops playing, and even ELLEN forgets to be angry for an instant.*) Enough, already! We haven't much time!

ELLEN. (*Moves angrily across toward piano.*) Don't worry! It'll only take me a minute to tear her hair out!

ILONA. (*As if reacting to the attitude and not the words, backs in fear toward DUNCAN as GLADYS rushes to intercept ELLEN.*) Que? Que dice, Duncan?

GLADYS. Ellen, don't! You've got to listen to me, *all* of you!

ILONA. (*DUNCAN has risen and comes around bench, fast, to face ELLEN, and she deftly keeps him between herself and his wife.*) Que? Que passe, Duncan?

GLADYS. (*Holding ELLEN back with one hand on her chest, turns head to snarl at ILONA:*) And you can cut out that bogus Berlitz bit, honey!

ELLEN. Bogus?! Gladys, what are you—?

ILONA. (*Startled, but sticking to her guns, prettily.*) Duncan, yo no comprendo su mujer—!

DUNCAN. *You* don't understand my wife?! What makes you think *I* do?!

GLADYS. Will you all shut up and—

**79**

ELLEN. (*Trying to get around* GLADYS.) Just let me get my hands on her—!

DUNCAN. Ellen, for the love of heaven—!

ILONA. *Que passe? No tiendo! Duncan, por que esta su mujer—?*

GLADYS. (*Before* ILONA *can finish her query, interrupts her with:*) Oh, keep your brassiere on! (*As* OTHERS *stare at her in shock, she adds, inspired:*) Though I'm surprised the *straps* can support all that *padding!*

ILONA. *Padding?!* Now, *listen,* sister—! (*Stops, biting her tongue in chagrin, but it is too late.*)

ELLEN. (*As* DUNCAN *goggles at* ILONA, *and* GLADYS *smiles in triumph.*) Dunc! She speaks English!

DUNCAN. Ilona! When did *you* learn *English?!*

ILONA. (*It's over; gives it up.*) In grammar school, if you must know!

DUNCAN. What?! But when I knew you in Valencia—

ELLEN. You knew Twinkletoes in Valencia?!

GLADYS. *Later!* Tell each other *later!*

ELLEN. B-but, Gladys—! If Dunc knew her—

DUNCAN. Never mind that! *I* want to know what went on behind the garbage truck with you and Bill!

ELLEN. *"Bill!"?* Bill who?

GLADYS. Bill Rutledge!

ELLEN. But *I* don't know Bill Rutledge! You're thinking of Sam Coleman.

DUNCAN. No, *you* were thinking of Sam Coleman, but you were dating Bill Rutledge!

ELLEN. Then—who's Sam Coleman?

GLADYS. Every able-bodied man on the U.S.S. Petoskey!

ILONA. Even Duncan was Sam Coleman when we first met. Of course, he told me the truth later on.

ELLEN. Well, I wish he'd lay a little of it on *me!*

GLADYS. Look, Bill's tattoo can't fascinate Bart Madden forever! You've got to listen to my plan, before both your reputations blow sky-high!

ELLEN. I don't *care* about my reputation!

GLADYS. But your career—

ELLEN. The hell with my career!

DUNCAN. Ellen! Darling! Do you really mean that?! *I* mean more to you than your career?

GLADYS. If you don't both shut up, *nobody's* going to have a career! When Bart Madden left his tape recorder on the *table,* he left his tape recorder *on!*

DUNCAN. Oh, no!

ELLEN. (*Means when he was near that recorder, earlier:*) What did you *say?!*

DUNCAN. What *didn't* I say! *Diego!* The *painting!* The *petticoats!* The *wedding—!*

ILONA. *My* painting?

GLADYS. Whose *petticoats?*

ELLEN. *What* wedding?!

DUNCAN. (*Sinks down onto piano bench, facing room, in despair.*) You'll read all about it in Mystique Magazine! (*Suddenly realizes, looks at* ILONA.) What do you mean—*your* painting?

ILONA. That's the whole reason I *came* here today! To beg you for the painting. Diego died penniless, but I thought—after all we'd been to each other—that maybe you could let me sell the painting, and that way I'd have enough money to start a little dancing school, and—

ELLEN. *What* wedding?!

DUNCAN. Ilona! Then—you didn't come here because of *me?* And those *promises?*

ILONA. Oh, Duncan, I know how you felt that day. I'd never hold you to those promises.

GLADYS. *What* promises?

ELLEN. What *wedding?!*

ILONA. But you see, Dunc, I couldn't *find* you when I came to New York, because you have an unlisted phone number, and the Spanish Consulate didn't know, either, but there was this man there who said he could help, and I didn't know he was a snooper

for Mystique Magazine, and he brought me to Bart
Madden, who promised to help me get the painting if
I'd play a little joke on you, and I didn't know you
had *another* wife, and—

ELLEN. *Another* wife? Dunc! You mean—you and
Ilona—?!

GLADYS. Congratulations! *Now* you know what
wedding!

ELLEN. (*Almost in tears.*) But Dunc—if you had a
wife—how could you and I—?

DUNCAN. I only *thought* I had! But there was one
small hitch: We couldn't get her husband's consent!

(*NOTE: Next 25 speeches are spoken without pause,
    picked up like lightning by each subsequent
    speaker, so that the total time involved is some-
    thing under 25 seconds.*)

ELLEN. Her husband was Diego Valdez!
ILONA. And he died!
ELLEN. When?
DUNCAN. It was in all the papers!
ELLEN. In the TV listings?
GLADYS. Of course not!
ELLEN. No wonder I missed it!
DUNCAN. He gave me the painting—
GLADYS. Dunc went to the cafe—
ILONA. He fell in love with you—
ELLEN. We came back here—
DUNCAN. And we got *really* married—
ELLEN. And you never told *me*—?
GLADYS. But with good *reason!*
ILONA. *What* reason?
DUNCAN. I was scared stiff!
ELLEN. Of *me?*
DUNCAN. Of *losing* you!
GLADYS. As for *Rosie*—
ELLEN. I never loved *Sam!*

DUNCAN. Then why did you *date* him?

ELLEN. A garbage collector dates *anybody!*

DUNCAN. Darling!

ELLEN. Darling! (*They embrace fervently, but with lightning speed, and then break, and join* ILONA *in turning swiftly to* GLADYS, *on:*)

ILONA, ELLEN, and DUNCAN. *Now, what's your plan?!* (*If the timing has been right, there will be applause here, so* GLADYS *can pause and get her thoughts in order, while the others hover anxiously waiting; then, as applause starts down from peak, and before it has had a chance to fade:*)

GLADYS. (*Beckons them all in close to her, speaking low and fast.*) We can't destroy the tape, or he'll *know* something's up and we can't *deny* what's on there, because it's too easy to check—

DUNCAN. So far, your plan is lousy.

GLADYS. Shut up and hear me out! But there's one thing we *can* do: Give the guy *more* information, *more* scandals, *more* secrets—

ELLEN. But we don't *have* any more . . . (*Eyes* DUNCAN *suddenly.*) At least, *I* don't—!

DUNCAN. Oh, Ellen—!

ILONA. Quiet, both of you, and listen to Gladys! I think *I* know what she's getting at! We hide all our needles in a haystack!

GLADYS. *Exactly!* We lay so much on this guy that the *real* secrets will sound like chicken feed, and get lost in the shuffle! He may not even *print* the real stuff!

ELLEN. But what happens when he prints the *phony* stuff?!

GLADYS. We say, "Prove it!" and sue Mystique Magazine for a million bucks!

ILONA. Wait a minute! How do we go about laying this false haystack on him?

GLADYS. I've cooked it all up with Marge, down at the switchboard. Here's how it works— Wait! I hear them! (ALL *suddenly straighten in apprehension.*) No time to explain, now! Just take your cue from me and Marge, and play along! Quick, everybody act natural! (*She dashes to sofa and almost leaps into a casual sitting stance on it,* DUNCAN *jumps to piano bench and poses with fingers on the keys and a soulful skyward look,* ILONA *leans sexily against the piano upstage of him, staring down at him as if in rapture, and* ELLEN· *wavers uncertainly at room center.*)

ELLEN. Gladys, what's *natural* for *me?!*

GLADYS. Your husband's got another woman—do what you'd do on your TV show! (BART, *then* BILL, *appear on stairs*—BART *toting the recorder and microphone—and come down into room, during:*)

BART. You ought to be ashamed of yourself, getting a thing like that on you!

BILL. It was an accident. I asked the man at the tattoo parlor for a *ferry* with a *tender* behind, and he didn't know I meant *boats!*

ELLEN. (*Overacting outrageously.*) Oh, Duncan, how could you?! I could forgive you about the woman—yes, even that—but all these years, why didn't you tell me about the *children?!* How many are there? No, don't tell me, I don't want to know! But— wait—that's not true. I *do* want to know. I'm just— afraid to know! Yet—somehow—I simply *must* know. . . ! (BART—*and even* BILL, *a bit, since he's not quite sure of the situation—are reacting visibly to all this.*)

DUNCAN. (*Callously, almost carelessly.*) Oh, okay. Thirteen. (ILONA *reacts, then recovers her nonchalance.*)

BART. *Thirteen?!* (*Conspirators all react as if they hadn't seen him there.*)

DUNCAN. (*Swiveling around on bench to face room, and standing.*) Well, two of them were adopted.

BILL. Dunc! I had no idea! Why didn't you tell me?

DUNCAN. (*Goes to him, clasps his hand.*) Because

you always said if I had any kids you wanted to be their godfather. I knew you couldn't afford it. (*Releases hand.*)

ELLEN. (*Rushes into a bewildered* BILL's *arms, head against his chest.*) Oh, Sam, Sam! Did you hear? Did you hear what he said? Thirteen children! Aren't you shocked?!

BILL. (*Unnoticed by* BART, *whose back is to her,* GLADYS *is giving* BILL *an it's-perfectly-all-right-so-play-along signal; he gets the message, puts his arms fondly around* ELLEN, *and:*) Yeah. *We've* only got seven!

BART. *Seven?!*

BILL. I spend a lot of time at sea. (*PHONE rings;* GLADYS *goes for it, but* BART *gallops there first.*)

BART. No-no, I'll get it, I'm expecting a call! (*Grabs up phone, meantime setting recorder on cocktail table.*) Hello . . . ? (*His expression changes at what he hears and echoes.*) "*Comrade Gladys*"?!

GLADYS. (*Grabs phone from him.*) Nonsense. You just misunderstood! (*Gets on phone, turns her back on him, but murmurs audibly:*) Da! . . . Nyet! . . . Da, tovarisch! . . . Da, da! . . . Nyet-Nyet! (*Hangs up, turning to him with innocent smile, on:*)

BART. Who was that?

GLADYS. Wrong number. (*BELL.*)

ELLEN. *I'll* get it! (*Disengages from* BILL, *opens door; a newspaper lies on floor.*) Oh, it's the New York Post! Why would Marge send *that* up—? (*As she gets it and lets door close again:*)

GLADYS. (*Hurries to her, and will take paper from her during:*) Because she knew none of us could leave to get it with our—visitor—here! (OTHERS *give* BART *a brief narrow-eyed scrutiny; he looks uneasy.*)

BART. What has my presence got to do with getting the newspaper?

OTHERS. *Nothing!* (*They are so vehement, he is now sure it means something.*)

GLADYS. (*Who has been thumbing as-if-frantically through paper.*) Ah, here it is! The review of Duncan's concert!

DUNCAN. (*As he and others—including an insanely curious* BART—*crowd in.*) Do they mention the mazurka—?!

GLADYS. (*Running finger down page.*) Mazurka—mazurka—mazurka— No! Not a word! There is no mention of your hesitation after the third bar!

BILL. Yet the Times mentioned it very specifically! So *that* means . . . !

BART. What? What does it mean?

GLADYS. (*As if he hadn't spoken, riffles quickly to new spot in paper.*) The shipping news! Duncan—how long was that hesitation—exactly?!

DUNCAN. Exactly two-and-one-half seconds. I practiced it for hours so I could do it without a timer!

ILONA. *Sehr gut, mein Herr!* (*And, as* BART *goggles at her sudden switchover to German:*)

ELLEN. *Ach, ja!*

BILL. *Du bist Wunderbar!*

DUNCAN. (*Shrugs off compliments modestly.*) *Mach nicht!*

GLADYS. (*Jabs finger at paper.*) Here it is! Third bar—that's pier three—two-and-one-half seconds—that's two-thirty this afteroon! The name of the ship is . . . the *Isaka Maru!*

BART. Wait a minute—Russian phone calls—German interjections—Japanese shipping— What's going *on* here?

OTHERS. *Nothing!*

DUNCAN. (*Inspired.*) The signal! It's time for the signal! (*Rushes and pulls drape-cord, re-exposing nightshirt.*)

BART. What's *that* doing there again?!

ELLEN. Is our man out in front of the armory—?!

BILL. (*Who has rushed to window, drapes opened, peers downward.*) Right on schedule! He got the signal!

DUNCAN. (*Now beside him at window, which a frantic* BART *is trying to look out of, over their shoulders.*) And there go the pigeons!

ELLEN. Which way are they headed?!

DUNCAN. (*As he and* BILL *turn back toward room.*) Toward the river!

GLADYS. That's perfect!

BART. Just a minute! Manhattan is an *island! All* directions are toward the river!

ILONA. Of course! That way, no one will be suspicious!

BART. Suspicious of *what?!*

OTHERS. *Nothing!*

BART. (*To* ILONA, *just realizing:*) Hey! You spoke English!

BILL. Why not? She's been speaking everything *else!*

BART. But she's not supposed to—that is—uh—I had no idea she could—

DUNCAN. Don't be ridiculous. All our agents speak at least six foreign tongues.

BART. Agents—?!

DUNCAN. (*Mildly.*) Did I say agents? I mean, friends.

BART. Then why did you say agents?

GLADYS. Well, most of his friends are agents.

ELLEN. (*To* BART, *as if covering up a bad slip.*) They mean *booking* agents, of course.

DUNCAN. (*As though realizing his slip and also covering.*) Uh—yes! Certainly! I play a lot of foreign countries.

ILONA. So they have to speak a lot of languages.

BILL. See how simple it is?

BART. (*Fumbles at pockets.*) Sure, sure I do. Hey, I can't find my camera! Where the hell—?! (OTHERS *get brief look of apprehension.*)

BILL. Maybe it fell out of your pocket while I was wrestling you into the upstairs bathroom . . .

BART. Yes! That must be it! Excuse me! Be right

back! Don't anybody leave! (*Exits up stairs at a gallop.*)

GLADYS. (*As* OTHERS *instantly converge about her.*) We can't let him take any pictures!

ILONA. I'll say we can't! We could all deny his *story* about the signal, and the armory and everything, but if he gets a *photograph* of us—!

BILL. (*Suavely, removing camera—a tiny mini-camera—from his pocket.*) Don't worry about a thing. I picked his pocket while we were wrestling. (*Pops it open, pockets film, closes it and tosses it over onto sofa, all during:*) We'll let him think he dropped it while he was recording. He won't get very good pictures without any film.

DUNCAN. Recording! That gives me an idea! (*He rushes to piano bench, opens it, grabs out cassette, rushes across room and swaps his cassette with the one in the recorder on cocktail table, chuckling evilly, during:*)

GLADYS. And I've got to call Marge and let her in on your improvisations! (*While she is dialing phone and* DUNCAN *is switching tapes:*)

BART. (*Off.*) I can't find it!

BILL. (*Calls up stairs.*) Look over near the perfume dispenser. That's where I finally pinned your shoulders to the bath mat!

ILONA. You know, I *thought* he smelled pretty good for a *reporter!*

GLADYS. (*On phone.*) Marge! It's me! Listen—call back in about one minute, say you're the armory, and ask which pigeon has the message on its leg! . . . Oh, and if you can swing it—use a Japanese accent!— Oops, I hear him! 'Bye, now! (*Hangs up, just as* DUNCAN *makes it back to piano bench with the tape from the machine and pops it inside;* BART *appears on stairs just as* DUNCAN *straightens and looks innocent.*)

BART. That camera's just *got* to be here! I *can't* have lost it!

ILONA. Why, what's so important about finding your camera—?

BART. (*Very uneasy, as others all turn and look at him as he continues frantic seach around room, under chairs, etc.*) Uh. Well. Some famous people aren't very long on brains. Once I figure I'm not going to get much in the way of repeatable quotations, I take a lot of pictures, instead. "Famous star looks out window . . . Famous star sits in favorite chair . . . Famous star scratches famous stomach . . ." (*It's all a nervous babble, and* OTHERS *immediately leap to take advantage of the inroads they're making on his nerves.*)

DUNCAN. *Who's* not long on brains?!

ELLEN. What do you *mean*, no repeatable quotations?!

GLADYS. Just what kind of pictures did you plan to *take?!*

BART. Uh. Well. It's this way— (*PHONE rings.*)

OTHERS. *I'll* get it! (*A stampede-sound ensues, but —since they all are fast-jogging in place, and he is the only one actually running—*BART *gets to the phone first and grabs it up.*)

BART. *Hello!* . . . Who? . . . (OTHERS *have all turned away, confident that this is* MARGE *on the line with the armory-story, so all react in fear when they hear:*) Oh, it's *you*, Sally! Didn't recognize your voice . . . *What* information? *I* asked you for—? . . . Good grief, I almost forgot. But look—uh— (*Senses* OTHERS *listening, turns partly away, lowers voice.*) Never mind that stuff now, I'm onto something much bigger—! . . . Oh, for pete's sake, Sally, I *know* I put you to a lot of trouble, but— Okay-okay, let's have it! . . . (*As he listens and speaks,* OTHERS *cringe in deep uneasiness.*) Sam Coleman is who—? The *chaplain?!* He *can't* be the chaplain, he's got *seven kids!* . . .

BILL. (*Conversationally.*) I couldn't help it, I was

crazed with desire. (*When* OTHERS—*excepting* BART, *who didn't hear him—look at him:*) Seven times.

BART. (*Still on phone.*) What? Who? "Rosie O'Reilly"? . . . And what's her connection with Ellen? . . . (OTHERS—*especially* ELLEN—*react, tense up, faces awaiting blow.*) But how *could* they lose her employment file?! . . . (OTHERS *grow more hopeful, listen eagerly as he listens; then:*) . . . Out with the garbage?!

BILL. (*As* ELLEN, GLADYS *and* DUNCAN *beam in delight, solemnly places his hand over his heart and intones:*) She would have *wanted* to go that way! (*Then his solemnity vanishes and he grins as* ELLEN *makes a fond oh-stop-clowning-you-loveable-idiot gesture at him, but then* ALL *return to tension and tune in again on* BART—*who has missed all this byplay behind him—as he continues:*)

BART. (*Still on phone to "Sally."*) Oh, never *mind* that! What've you got on this Bill Rutledge? . . . (*As he echoes information aloud,* BILL *will automatically do a physical denial of the description, as follows:*) About six feet tall . . . (BILL *knee-bends himself shorter.*) Quite good-looking . . . (BILL *contorts face into misshapen ugliness.*) Healthy and athletic . . . (BILL *hunches back, gnarls hands, starts leg-dragging limp in direction of maid's-room, but* BART *has casually turned his head at this point, notices, and yips, off phone:*) Hey, what's the matter with *him?* (BILL *snaps up from misshapen position, during:*)

OTHERS. *Nothing!*

BART. But—?! (*Suddenly returns to phone, as he hears something, and* BILL *will give it up, straighten, and rejoin group, during:*) What? Who is this? . . . What operator? You've cut into a very important call! . . . The *armory—?!* (*Covers phone, addresses group.*) Some lady with a Japanese accent calling from the armory next door—!

GLADYS. So take a message!

BART. (*Back on phone.*) Can I take a message? (*Listens, and repeats what he hears.*) "Which *pigeon* has the *message* on its leg?! . . . *Boris* has to know?!"

GLADYS. Tell her it's the gray-and-black pigeon with the missing toenail!

BART. (*Baffled but cooperative, on phone.*) The gray-and-black one with the missing toenail. . . . (*Then realizes what he's done, shouts to no one in particular:*) Hey, what am I *doing?!* . . . Hello? *Hello?!* (*Jiggles cutoff in vain, hangs up.*) What was all *that* about?!

ELLEN. What does it matter? The point is, now you're an accessory!

OTHERS. (*Opens arms to him as if in welcome.*) *Comrade!*

BART. (*Reacts in horror.*) Now just a minute—! I only—I never—she asked—so I simply—! Now just a minute!

GLADYS. Don't be nervous. You'll *enjoy* being a fugitive from the law!

DUNCAN. *We* certainly do!

BART. B-but—but—! Good grief, this is horrible! (*Lurches to cocktail table, reaches for his drink.*)

ELLEN. (*Before it quite reaches his lips.*) No, don't! It's poisoned!

BART. Poisoned?! But—you and I switched glasses! I *made* you switch!

DUNCAN. But she knew you would!

BART. (*In shock, gets glass back on cocktail table, stares at it.*) Why—why did you *stop* me—?!

ILONA. Because *now* you're one of *us!*

BART. What? You're crazy!

BILL. You relayed the message to Boris. We'll all testify to that. When the *Isaka Maru* goes down—

BILL and OTHERS. (*Shrug in unison.*) Wellll . . . !

BART. But I didn't know what I was doing—! (*PHONE rings.*)

OTHERS. *I'll* get it!

BART. (*Same jog-in-place for group as* BART *gallops madly to phone; he grabs it up.*) Hello! Sally! Listen, quickly—no-no, the hell with Bill Rutledge! . . . (BILL *looks slightly miffed, but lets it go, during:*) Call the Port Authority! Have them stop the Isaka Maru from sailing at two-thirty today! Seach the ship for a man named Boris! They'll recognize him by the gray-and-black pigeon! . . . I have *not* gone crazy! (OTHERS, *after a look at one another, decide that their obvious attitude should be contrary to what he's doing, so they all start toward him at this point, overlapping speeches:*)

DUNCAN. Grab that phone!

ILONA. Cut the wires!

GLADYS. We've been betrayed!

ELLEN. Stop him!

BILL. He'll ruin everything! (*The overlap conveys their—apparent—feelings, though the nearly simultaneous delivery will make it sound like urgent gibberish; however, all speeches cease together as* BART *whips an automatic pistol out of his coat and covers them, all their hands going ceilingward, as they ad-lib yelps of dismay, and show quite genuine apprehension, as* BART *continues on phone:*)

BART. (*Arcing pistol back and forth horizontally to keep them at bay.*) That's right, Sally! . . . Never mind how dopey it sounds, do it! (*Hangs up, advancing toward them, as they back uneasily away.*) Now we're going to get to the bottom of this thing!

ELLEN. Do all magazine reporters carry *artillery* on the job?!

BART. They do at *Mystique* Magazine!

GLADYS. If they want to get back to their typewriters *alive!*

BART. (*Gestures with gun.*) Stand where you are, all of you! (*They stop backing, but keep hands high.*)

Ilona! You get over there to that phone and call the police! And don't try any tricks!

ILONA. (*Semi-lowering hands, takes an uncertain step phoneward.*) Why—why should *I* help you—?

BART. Because the crime here is treason. As a non-citizen, you may get off with a simple deportation; these others are headed for a federal prison! Now, move!

ILONA. (*Nearly in tears, moving past him toward phone.*) B-but—I don't *want* to be deported! I'm sick of singing in that stupid cafe! I want to settle down in America with a nice little dancing school!

BART. You should have *thought* of that before you hitched your wagon to a *red star!*

GLADYS. Hey, you really know how to turn a catchy phrase.

BART. (*Modestly, almost forgetting what he's doing.*) Aw, well, when you've been writing as long as *I* have— (OTHERS *had relaxed when he did, but all hands go high again as he remembers himself and jabs pistol at them, on:*) Hold it! Not another word out of any of you! Ilona—make that call!

ILONA. (*Wavers, beside phone, then sees drink on table, gets flash of inspiration, grabs it up in her hand.*) No! No! They'll never take me alive! (*Drains drink, gasps, clutches throat, drops glass onto table.*)

ELLEN. (*Rushes to her.*) Ilona!

DUNCAN. (*To* BART, *as he rushes over to* ILONA *with* GLADYS.) *Now* see what you've done!

BILL. (*Solemnly shaking his head.*) She was so young . . . so sweet . . . so innocent . . . and, boy, was she stacked!

BART. (*Babbling with horror, pistol waggling between* BILL *and* OTHERS.) How did *I* know she'd do a dumb stunt like that?!

GLADYS. (*Accusingly, as she,* ELLEN *and* DUNCAN *support "dying" girl.*) What *other* choice did you leave her, you heartless wretch?! (*PHONE rings.*)

OTHERS. *I'll* get it! (*Same business, as* BART *goes for it, keeping them covered.*)

BART. Hello?! . . . Sally! . . . *What?!* . . . But it *must* be there! . . . Are you sure? . . . Yeah. Yeah. Okay . . . (*Hangs up, dazed, addresses group in perplexity.*) She said there's no such ship in port, and no two-thirty sailing from *any* of the piers today . . . ?!

DUNCAN. Well, the New York Post isn't absolutely *perfect* . . . *!*

GLADYS. Yeah, they never noticed what you did to that mazurka. (*Gets a dirty look from* DUNCAN, *during:*)

ILONA. Oh! The pain! I'm going! I'm *going!* It is a far, far better thing—! (*Suddenly slumps in their grip, "dead."*)

BILL. What is?

DUNCAN. (*As he,* ELLEN *and* GLADYS *lower* ILONA *onto sofa.*) She didn't say. (*PHONE rings;* BART *starts for it, looks in pause of puzzlement at immobile* OTHERS; *they instantly jog in place, and he lurches to phone and grabs it.*)

BART. *Hello?!*—Sally! Listen, I have no time to talk, now. Just forget all that stuff I asked you for, something more important's come up!

GLADYS. Yeah, like being an accessory to murder! Driving a person to suicide's the same as killing them!

BART. (*Covers mouthpiece.*) Who, *me?* What are you talking about?!

GLADYS. Your contract with Ilona. It proves you sent her here. When the police find her body—

OTHERS. (*Shrug in unison on:*) Wellll . . . !

BART. Good grief, you're right! (*On phone:*) Sally! Get the Valdez agreement—all existing copies—and burn it! . . . Never *mind* the company regulations, just *do* it! . . . Because I don't have *time* to get the publisher's approval! Believe me, he'll *thank* me for it! Now get that file to the incinerator, quick, and stop *calling* me here! (*Slams down phone, waves trio away from "corpse" back to stand with* BILL, *below elevator door, using gun for emphasis.*) Now, get over there, all of you! I warn you, one false move and you're dead! I'm sending for the police! (*As he reaches for phone with his free hand, PHONE rings; he jumps in reaction, then wails:*) Aargh! Can't that stupid girl obey orders?! (*Grabs up phone.*) Now, listen, Sally—! . . . What? . . . (*Holds mouthpiece to chest, asks group:*) Who is Mrs. Kramer?

ELLEN. Why—she's the lady in the apartment down-stairs. Her husband works nights—maybe we were making too much racket . . .

BART. (*Back on phone.*) Listen, Mrs. Kramer, I'm sorry if we were making a racket, but— . . . Then what *did* you call about? . . . *Who?* . . . (*Looks puzzled, glances suspiciously at* GLADYS; *then, on phone:*) Yes, she's here . . . She's fine . . . *Okay* . . . !?

ILONA. (*Raises head.*) *Que?* (*Others shush her before* BART *turns.*)

BART. (*Blinking in confusion.*) She wanted to know if Gladys made it safely up the fire escape. (*To* GLADYS, *at sea:*) What were you doing on the *fire escape?*

GLADYS. (*Glances windowward, sees nightshirt, gets inspiration.*) Trying to get that nightshirt before it was too late! But that narrow ledge made me lose my nerve.

BILL. (*Senses she's up to something, helps her along.*) What's so important about the nightshirt?

GLADYS. Our orders are in the pocket!

DUNCAN. (*As he and* ELLEN *catch on, picks up the ball.*) Our *secret* orders? From the *chief?!*

ELLEN. Oh, Gladys, why did you put them in the *nightshirt?!*

GLADYS. I thought they'd be safe there. No one in their right mind would go out on that ledge to have a look!

BART. Then why did you try to go out there and get them back?

GLADYS. Because *you* were here, of course! You were catching on, fast! I knew it was only a matter of minutes before all was lost! I *had* to get them, with the chief's secret *identity* on them!

DUNCAN. And just because you're afraid of heights, you *left* them there?!

GLADYS. I'm sorry . . . !

ELLEN. You fool! You've ruined everything!

BILL. And you know the penalty for failure!

GLADYS. No-no! Not that! Anything but that!

BART. Anything but *what?* What *is* the penalty for failure?

DUNCAN. It's so horrible the *chief* won't even *tell* us!

BART. Gosh!

GLADYS. (*Falls to her knees before trio, wringing her hands.*) Oh, please, isn't there something I can do? Some way to make it up? Don't make me pay the penalty! Don't!

DUNCAN. (*Very ominously.*) There is—*one* way . . . !

GLADYS. (*Rocks back on her heels, looking horrified.*) No-no! Not that! Anything but that!

ELLEN. (*Casually, to* BART:) Some days there's just no pleasing her.

BILL. Enough of this foolishness! *You* know what you must do, Gladys! Do *it!*

BART. *What? What* must she do?

DUNCAN. Go out on that ledge—

ELLEN. Take the orders from the pocket—

BILL. Chew them up and swallow them—

GLADYS. (*Sobs.*) Then jump to my death! (*Flops sideways from knees onto floor.*)

BART. That's horrible! You three just *stand* there, while this poor woman plunges shrieking to the *pavement—?!*

DUNCAN. *Stand* here?

BILL. Of course not!

ELLEN. We sing "Hail to the Chief"!

BART. Are there *words* to that?

DUNCAN. Well, we use the Moscow lyrics. (*BELL; all look toward elevator door.*)

BART. Who's that?!

BILL. (*To* GLADYS.) Are we expecting anybody?

GLADYS. (*Sits up on floor.*) Only that certain—package . . . !

BART. Aha! Now we're getting someplace! (*Keeping gun ready, whips open door; package—about the size of a hatbox—lies on floor; he picks it up by its twine binding, lets door close, holds package high.*) And what have we here?! (*Holds it to his ear.*) It's—it's ticking!

GLADYS. (*Leaps to her feet.*) Be careful with that, you idiot! It's the time-bomb!

BART. (*Backsteps, unnerved.*) Time-bomb?!

GLADYS. For Carnegie Hall, tonight!

ELLEN. At forty-seven minutes after nine o'clock!

BART. But why?! Why would you blow up Carnegie Hall?!

GLADYS. Because at nine-forty-seven, the President of the United States will be passing almost directly underneath Carnegie Hall on the Seventh Avenue Subway, on his way to the Columbus Circle Station!

BART. You fiends! You monsters! (*Sets package gingerly on chess table.*) Thank heaven I showed up here today! It's all falling into place! The Duncan Latimer concert at Carnegie Hall tonight is nothing but an excuse for this traitorous scheme! You pretend you're going there to play—but you're really going there to bomb!

ELLEN. (*Gets extremely dirty look from* DUNCAN *as she observes:*) I guess he's heard the mazurka.

BART. Well, you're not getting away with it, any of you! Stand back and keep your hands up! I'm going out there and getting that nightshirt!

BILL. No, you can't do that! (OTHERS *stare at him in surprise.*) While you're out there, they'll all get away!

BART. You're right! I didn't think of that! Okay, I'll force one of *them* to go out and get it!

BILL. (*As* OTHERS *give him looks of dismay and confusion, since he seems to be lousing up their scheme to get* BART *away.*) No, you can't do that, either! Whoever got the nightshirt would take it right down the fire escape and you'd *never* find out who the chief was!

BART. Good heavens! I didn't think of that, either! . . . Say—! How come you're being so helpful to me, all of a sudden?

DUNCAN. (*Hands going to hips, as he asks in angry sincerity:*) Yeah, how come?!

BILL. (*Will step forward one pace toward* BART, *and salute, during:*) Because, in reality, I am— Commander Bill Rutledge, of Naval Secret Service! (OTHERS *fling hands out, and do a unified gasp-reaction of "shock."*)

BART. Bill Rutledge! Of course! Sally's description fits you like a glove! But wait—how do I know this isn't a trick?!

BILL. May I reach in my pocket?

BART. All right—but very carefully—!

BILL. (*Produces wallet, flips it open.*) My I.D. card! See for yourself! (BART *leans forward, reads card, his eyes widen, and as he straightens again,* BILL *re-pockets wallet briskly.*)

BART. You *are* Bill Rutledge! Then what was this Sam Coleman bit?!

BILL. That was my cover! I had orders to infiltrate this organization, seek out the identity of the chief, and then turn everybody in to the feds!

DUNCAN. You traitor!

GLADYS. You liar!

ELLEN. You swine!

BART. (*Gun-waves them all away from* BILL, *upon whom they seemed ready to converge with murderous intent.*) Stand back! Leave him alone! Bill—the chief's identity—do you know it?!

BILL. No, but it's right out there, waiting for us—
if the *wind* doesn't blow that nightshirt *away—!*

BART. There's no time to lose! Here—! (*Hands
pistol to* BILL.) You keep them all covered! I'll go
get the nightshirt! (BILL *points gun at group, they all
raise their hands, and* BART *dashes off toward maid's-
room; instantly, they drop their hands and sag in relief; but:*)

BILL. No you don't! Get those hands back up!
Quick! (*Dumbfounded, they all do, staring at him,
including* ILONA, *who started sitting up the moment*
BART *disappeared.*)

GLADYS. What is this, a doublecross?!

DUNCAN. Good grief! What if he's the *real* Bill
Rutledge and we're all *trapped!?*

ELLEN. (*Turns incredulous look upon him; then:*)
Dunc—are you nuts? None of us is *really* a spy!

DUNCAN. (*Blinking.*) Oh, yeah. I forgot. But Bill—
what the hell—?! (*Starts to lower hands and step
forward, but gets them up again when* BILL *gun-
gestures him back into place.*)

BILL. Shut up and let me explain!

GLADYS. But we've got to get *out* of here!

BILL. Yes, but don't you understand, I can't simply
*let* you go! We've taken care of Ilona's *problem*—the
contracts are burnt to a cinder by now—but we've
still got to get her *out* of here!

ELLEN. But—what do you want us to *do?!*

BILL. Just stand there, with your hands up, so
everything looks okay when he gets outside that window. Then I want you to jump me, get the gun—

DUNCAN. And bump you off! Of course!

BILL. Not *really*, Dunc! But—

GLADYS. Jiggers! I think he's almost there! Quiet,
everybody! (ILONA *"dies" again.*)

ELLEN. He can't hear us out there. The traffic noises
are deafening!

BILL. You're right! But whatever you say, keep on
making the thing *look* good! (BART *appears on ledge,*

*inching toward nightshirt;* BILL *sees him, turns his head and waves;* OTHERS *instantly jump him, wrestle him to floor, while* BART *watches in horror;* DUNCAN *pins one arm, pries pistol from his fingers, while* ELLEN *sits on his other arm, and* GLADYS *squats on his chest and proceeds to "strangle" him, laughing fiendishly.)* That's it! Keep it up! Then—the moment I'm knocked unconscious—the rest of you get out of here and cook up alibis! (BART *will continue to stare in horror till further notice.)*

ELLEN. I can rejoin that party at the V.F.W. hall!

DUNCAN. *I* can get the manager at Carnegie Hall to swear I've been there practicing all afternoon—! (BILL *is meanwhile writhing, kicking heels on floor, etc., as they "choke" and "punch" him.)*

GLADYS. I can go get mugged in Central Park!

BILL. Perfect!

GLADYS. (*Sees* BART, *finally broken from his shocked inertia, grab the nightshirt and start back toward maid's-room.*) Oh, damn, he's coming! Let's get out of here! (*Trio leaves* BILL *on floor, rushes to door; it won't open.*)

DUNCAN. *Damn* this stupid elevator! (*Jabs button;* ILONA *sits up.*)

ILONA. What about *me?*

BILL. (*Supine on floor.*) Lie down and stay dead! I've got it all worked out!

ILONA. But—

ELLEN. He'll be here any second! What'll we do?!

GLADYS. Upstairs, quick! Follow me! (*As if leading a cavalry charge, she flees up stairs,* DUNCAN *and* ELLEN *fleeing after her;* BILL *waves at* ILONA.)

BILL. Down, girl, *down!* (*She rolls her eyes heavenward in exasperation, but "dies" again, and* BILL *slumps limply just as* BART *dashes in with nightshirt in his grasp; he drops to his knees beside* BILL.)

BART. Bill! Bill! Are you all right?! I saw everything! Those dirty cowards! Say something! Speak to me! (*BELL; he jumps to his feet, grabbing up pistol which has been left on floor beside* BILL; *yanks door open.*) Aha! (*Then realizes.*) Nobody there! But they didn't have time to get to the ground floor before I came in—so they must still be here! (*Waving pistol before him, he dashes up stairs; almost immediately,* DUNCAN, ELLEN *and* GLADYS *gallop in from kitchen, as* BILL *sits up on floor.*)

BILL. (*Quietly.*) You'd better hurry. He seems awfully upset. (DUNCAN *grabs doorknob; door won't open; he screams in rage.*)

DUNCAN. Ellen, if it's the last thing we do, we're moving to another apartment!

ELLEN. I'm getting a little tired of this death-trap, myself!

DUNCAN. Darling! You mean that?! I can finally get my Steinway out of storage?!

ELLEN. As long as our new apartment has at *least* seventeen *exits!* But first, tell me one thing—

DUNCAN. What?

ELLEN. How do you know Gladys is ticklish?

GLADYS. Will you settle your domestic problems some other time and push that stupid button?!

DUNCAN. Oh, sorry. (*Jabs button; an instant later, we hear* BART *on stairs.*) Yipe! Here he comes again! Come on! (ALL *gallop out into kitchen,* BILL *and* ILONA—*who naturally sat up to listen to them—instantly flop down again;* BART *descends two steps at a time into room, stops, looks about, then starts for kitchen; BELL; he rocks to a halt, turns and yanks door open; empty; he growls incoherently, then gallops out into kitchen; an instant later, the fugitives come tumbleleaping down stairs,* DUNCAN *grabs doorknob, and this time the door comes open instantly.*) Bingo! (ELLEN, GLADYS, *and* DUNCAN *leap aboard, and* DUNCAN *tries to shut door, but* GLADYS *stops him, and leans out toward* BILL.)

GLADYS. Hey—that party's big enough for two

more—how'd you like to meet me over at the V.F.W. hall as soon as you've cleared out of here?!

BILL. You've got yourself a date! That sounds like fun.

GLADYS. Well, it beats getting mugged in Central Park! Besides, I want a look at that tattoo—!

DUNCAN. *Will* you get *in* here—?! (*It is a near-scream of frustration, so she does, and he slams door, as* BILL *and* ILONA *flop down again and* BART *comes dashing madly into room from kitchen; his hair is a mess, his clothes are rumpled, his face sliding down, door-crack as he "tracks elevator," on:*)

BART. Wait! Stop! Come back here! (*Then:*) It's no use . . . they got away . . . I don't know how they did it, but they got away . . . (*Straightens suddenly, as* BILL *moans and sits up.*) Bill! You're alive! (*Rushes to him, helps him to his feet.*) Thank heaven you're okay! I thought they'd done for you, for sure!

BILL. (*As if dazed and reeling.*) What—what happened—where are they—? Good grief, you didn't let them get *away?!*

BART. (*Lifts nightshirt into his view.*) Yes, but don't worry! I have the secret identity of the chief!

BILL. Wonderful! Your country will never forget you for this! Who is he?!

BART. (*Pulls small bit of paper from nightshirt pocket, reads aloud:*) "Inspected by Number Twenty-One"—! (*Realizes suddenly what he has; drops it, groans.*) Oh, no! No-no-no! It was all a trick, to get me out of here, so they could jump you, and make their getaway! We'll never get them now!

BILL. No! Wait! There's just one slim chance—! (*Starts toward sofa.*) If I can get her to a hospital, in time, they may be able to revive her! She can turn state's evidence in exchange for her freedom! (*Pulls a limp* ILONA *to her feet, gets her across his shoulder in a fireman's carry, calls out to* BART:) Ring for that elevator! (*Adds sincerely:*) Hurry! She's heavier than I thought!

BART. (*Dazzled by events, turns and obediently pushes button; meantime, on* BILL'S *shoulder,* ILONA—*behind* BART'S *back, of course—calls his attention to portrait on wall, then will slump again before* BART *turns around.*) Elevator! Yes! Hospital! State's evidence! We'll get them yet!

BILL. (*As* BART *turns, and* ILONA *feigns death again.*) One thing more! That picture! I'd better take it with me! It'll *prove* our case against the Latimers!

BART. Picture! Of course! (*Rushes to picture, which he will take from wall, as* BILL *totes* ILONA *over to elevator;* BART *will follow after them, carrying picture under his àrm.*) That will prove everything! The doctors see her, they see the picture, and immediately they know that—that—? (*Stops right behind* BILL, *stymied.*) *What* will they know? What does the *picture* prove?

BILL. That Duncan knew Ilona back in Valencia before he married Ellen, of course! Isn't that obvious?! (*BELL;* BILL *immediately grabs knob, opens door, enters elevator with* ILONA—*her upper torso hanging over his back—now the nearest one to* BART.)

BART. Oh, yes, of course! (*Holds out picture.*)

ILONA. (*Lifts face, smiles, takes picture from* BART.) Here, *I'll* carry that, he's got his hands full! (BART *obediently hands picture to her, she takes it in one hand, then pulls door shut with the other, on:*) Adios, muchacho!

BART. Adios! (*As door slams in his face, suddenly realizes.*) Hey, she's alive! (*Same slide on:*) Wait! Stop! Come back here! (*PHONE rings; he screams:*) I'll get it! (*Runs halfway there; realizes there's no need; then calmly walks rest of way across room and answers it, quietly:*) Hello—? . . . (*Then, very excited again:*) Oh! Yes, sir! Madden here! . . . What? . . . Oh, but there wasn't any *time* to get your authorization, boss, before the contracts were destroyed . . . Well, you see, with the dead girl here— (*Suddenly casts bewildered glance toward elevator; then:*) At

least, I *thought* she was dead, but—! . . . Sir, you've
got to hear me out! I have enough evidence here to—
well, just listen to *this!* (*Brings phone to recorder,
holds receiver near speaker area, then presses "Play"
button; immediately, we hear a multi-banjo rendition
of* "Camptown Races"; BART *reacts, and after about
ten seconds of the theme, he presses "Stop" button, and
lifts phone slowly and wearily to his head again.*)
What? . . . Oh. Yes, I guess that *was* a little
flat . . . But you see, sir—I thought there was a—
. . . No, I have *not* been drinking! And lucky
I wasn't, because the drink was so full of poison
—at least, they *said* it was full of poison—well,
look, let me explain—there was this red nightshirt
outside the window, and when the pigeons took off
from the armory, naturally I thought the *Isaka
Maru* was going to be sunk, so—but later, when the
time-bomb arrived—sir? . . . *Sir?!* . . . (*Sighs, hangs
up; stands there, looks toward package on chess table;
wanders over there, listlessly, snaps twine, opens lid,
and a half-dozen coil-spring-and-fabric "snakes"
jump out ceilingward; he has momentarily yelped, but
now he quietly recovers, lifts large ticking alarm-
clock from box, sighs, puts it back in, then stares
thoughtfully and dejectedly out front, and remarks
wearily:*) I wonder if Harvey Spoonbill could use a
roommate?"

*CURTAIN*

## PROPERTY LIST

*(NOTE: Since the action of the play is continuous, with no gap in time between acts, the "Preset" items should all be in place from the top of the show, which should make things easier on the stage manager than having to run his/ her checklist prior to each act.)*

Preset—
Cup of coffee for Duncan at top of show, "Camptown Races" cassette inside piano bench, "Inspected by—" paper in pocket of movable nightshirt (see "RECOMMENDATIONS").

ACT ONE: *Worn, held, or carried on by—*

DUNCAN:
Original cup of coffee, refilled cup of coffee, bagful of liquor bottles, wristwatch (after dressing), scotch on the rocks (3 times)

GLADYS:
Purse containing large plane-ticket envelope and wads of crumpled bills, a New York Times, suitcase, open bottle of Coca Cola, coffee in cup with saucer

ELLEN:
Key to elevator door (suit should have pockets, for putting key and—later—money received from Gladys)

BILL:
Suitcase, wrapped cookbook, "little black book" in trouser pocket, scotch on the rocks (twice)

ILONA:
Two suitcases

ACT TWO:

BART:
Shoulder-slung cassette recorder with microphone and with cassette inside recorder, small notepad with pencil or pen, scotch on the rocks

105

BILL:
  Mug of coffee, coffeepot

GLADYS:
  Boxed chess set

ILONA:
  Nightshirt

ELLEN:
  Her own scotch on the rocks, later both her and Bart's scotches on the rocks

DUNCAN:
  Nightshirt from ledge, scotch on the rocks

ACT THREE:

BILL:
  Wallet in pocket, minicamera with film-pack in pocket

BART:
  Automatic pistol in pocket, nightshirt from ledge

STAGE MANAGER:
  New York Post, then "snake" box, must be set at proper time inside elevator door

SOUND EFFECTS:
  Pre-taped segment of "LUST FOR LIFE" with voice of ELLEN, voice of ANNOUNCER (actor portraying "BART" can do this), and plaintive ORGAN music; PHONE bell; BELL (with simultaneous light-flash from box) over elevator door; optional additional sound can be a loud BUZZ whenever anyone presses elevator button, if desired for contrast with other sound effects; pre-taped banjo-rendition of "Camptown Races."

COSTUME:
  USN Commander's Uniform for Bill

## RECOMMENDATIONS

1) Use a "DUNCAN" who actually can play the piano. Playing can be faked, of course, with tape-recordings or even an offstage pianist whose instrument is miked to a speaker inside a false spinet on the set, but a non-player never looks right or moves right when playing, and the stop/ start bits with the mazurka could come off quite badly if the timing was even fractionally off.

2) Use two identical nightshirts. The reason for this is that things seldom fall or flop where you want them to, so the shirt that twice appears outside the window should be permanently fastened by its cuff, and also wired or cardboarded so that it will always flop into a position where the monogram can be seen. Each time the drapes are drawn, of course, the permanently affixed nightshirt is drawn up out of sight, and the movable nightshirt is hung there for removal first by Duncan, later by Bart, and this will be the shirt seen when the drapes re-open each time.

3) The imaginary "television set" is in order to prevent blockage of sight lines for the audience. If your theater, however, is one with a stage that is below the level of the audience, then by all means use an actual set for more realism, as long as its presence will not block the spectators' view of the performance. In either case, do not relocate the set elsewhere onstage; its positioning is deliberate, because it accounts, therefore, for the positioning of the armchairs, which are there solely to keep Duncan and Bill in a downfront position for their drinking-and-exposition scene in Act One. Without a television there, the positioning of the armchairs is unnatural, and would subliminally bother the audience.

107

## NOTES FROM THE PREMIERE PRODUCTION

- The Country Club Players opted to use an actual TV set—
  a very small portable (about 6″ x 8″ x 10″) —on the
  coffee table for the opening of the show, and then Duncan
  took it with him when he went upstairs to dress, leaving
  the table clear for, later, the cookbook, the recorder, the
  "time-bomb," assorted drinks, etc.

- For the chess scene, Gladys brought Bill onstage, then took
  the already-set table-and-chessboard from elevator area,
  and arranged it so that the players sat on the hassock and
  in the armchair, with the pre-set table between them. Later
  in the act, when Gladys jumps up from her not-yet-started
  game with Bill, worried about what Ellen may say to Bart
  in the interview, Bill simply cleared the table and put it
  back where it had been, near the elevator, to open up the
  staging area for subsequent dashing about, etc.

- For the "hiding" scene, Gladys went behind piano.

- When the "time-bomb" arrived, the Players opted to have
  a panicky Bart (right after Gladys said it was a time-
  bomb) toss it to Duncan, who in turn tossed it to Bill, who
  tossed it to Gladys, who tossed it to Ellen, who then sent
  it similarly to Bill, to Duncan, and back to Bart, who turned
  in panic to send it to someone else—except, of course, no
  one was there to toss it to—so then he very carefully set it
  down upon the coffee table during his "You fiends! . . ."
  speech.

- The phone had a very long cord, so that the final time
  Bart answered it, he could bring it down to the coffee table
  where the recorder was left.

- Optional lines: At bottom of p. 53, as BART and ELLEN
  entered down aisle, from "upstairs"—
  BART. Thanks for the tour. I especially enjoyed your garbage
  compacter.
  ELLEN. You have no idea how easy that makes life for
  garbage collectors!

Piano Score for use in "TAKE A NUMBER, DARLING"

Mazurka in B Flat:

(pause - repeat;
pause - repeat;
pause - then do:)

Camptown Races:

(stop here
on sound
of BELL)

Mexican Hat Dance: (Act II - repeat till curtain; Act III - till "Okay!")

Ole!

Ole!

Ole!
(Okay!)

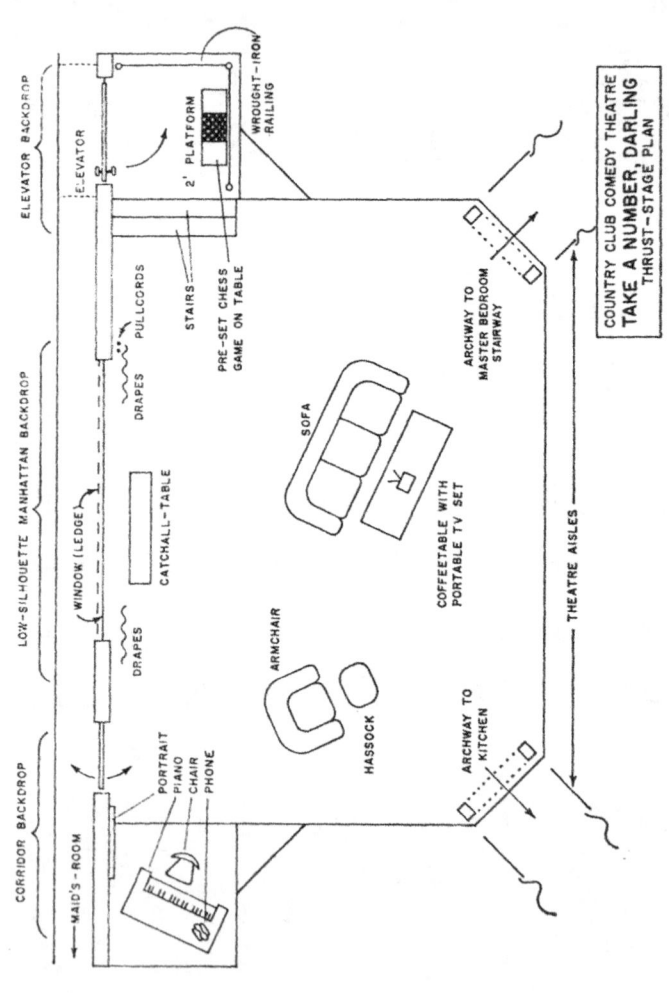

ELEVATOR BACKDROP

ELEVATOR

WROUGHT-IRON
RAILING

2' PLATFORM

STAIRS

PRE-SET CHESS
GAME ON TABLE

DRAPES PULLCORDS

LOW-SILHOUETTE MANHATTAN BACKDROP

WINDOW (LEDGE)

CATCHALL-TABLE

DRAPES

SOFA

COFFEETABLE WITH
PORTABLE TV SET

ARCHWAY TO MASTER BEDROOM
STAIRWAY

ARMCHAIR

HASSOCK

THEATRE AISLES

CORRIDOR BACKDROP

MAID'S-ROOM

PORTRAIT
PIANO
CHAIR
PHONE

ARCHWAY TO
KITCHEN

COUNTRY CLUB COMEDY THEATRE
TAKE A NUMBER, DARLING
THRUST-STAGE PLAN

110

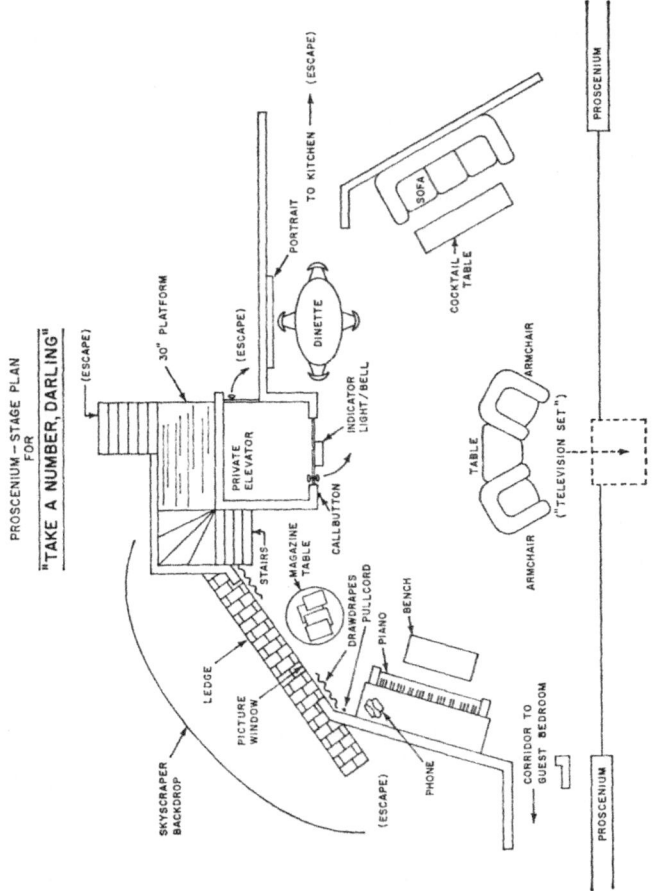

PROSCENIUM—STAGE PLAN
FOR
"TAKE A NUMBER, DARLING"